THE WALLFLOWER'S WILD WAGER

Ladies of Opportunity
A Bluestockings and Rogues Opposites Attract Regency
Mystery Christmas Romance

Book One

By
Collette Cameron®

Sweet-to-Spicy Timeless Romance ®

HUMAN
AUTHORED
AG Authors Guild
1413975

Attn: Permissions Coordinator
Blue Rose Romance® **LLC**
collette@collettecameronbooks.com
collettecameron.com

eBook ISBN: 978-1-966087-14-4
Print Book ISBN: 978-1-966087-15-1

FREE BOOK!

JOIN MY EXCLUSIVE MAILING LIST
Collette Cameron Newsletter

AND GET A FREE EBOOK!

https://collettecameronbooks.com/freegift

Plus Sneak Peeks, Giveaways, Contests, Exclusive Content, and More… P.S. I promise only good stuff ~ **no** spam!

DEDICATION

For Dee—my soul-sister.

ACKNOWLEDGMENTS

To my amazing assistant, Dee Foster, thank you for everything that you do to keep me sane. Praises to Shannon Gilmore for the breathtaking cover.

THE WALLFLOWER'S WILD WAGER

A Regency Mystery & Suspense Christmas Romance

LADIES OF OPPORTUNITY
BOOK ONE

COLLETTE CAMERON®

CONTENTS

ONE

Gloucester Street, London

I'm late. Again.

Without waiting for the aging driver to climb down, lower the step, and wrench open the outdated coach's door, Aubriella Penford agilely hopped from the conveyance just as it rolled to a stop before the Danforths' unobtrusive townhome in the quasi-fashionable London neighborhood.

The hot coals inside the foot warmer had done little to alleviate the vehicle's chill, yet the frigid air slapping her cheeks upon her descent onto the pavement caused her to inhale sharply. Huddled into her new raspberry-red and black redingote—how Aubriella adored the vibrant shade—she shivered as she waved Mosely back to his seat.

"No need to come down, Mosely."

The sooner she was inside, the sooner he could find himself a cozy table in Ye Olde Cheshire Cheese pub and enjoy a pint or two while flirting with Widow Waddell.

Aubriella darted a swift glance toward the house, unsurprised to see a yellowed lace curtain pushed aside and Roxina Danforth peering at the lane. A wry smile curving her mouth, she fluttered her fingers at Aubriella before permitting the panel to fall into place once more. Likely so that she could tell the others that Aubriella had finally arrived.

Against her will, her attention slid to the equally unremarkable but tidy brick townhouse next door before she jerked it away. The Matherfield brothers lived there. Jackson Matherfield, the eldest and a close friend of her brother's, had been a sharp, irritating pebble in her shoe for the better part of fifteen years.

Aubriella tightened her jaw, vexed at her lack of self-control as much as her continual lack of punctuality.

She loathed making her friends wait, but escaping the house wasn't easy. Mama must be informed and approve of Aubriella's use of the coach. Jessamine, her seventeen-year-old sister, often begged to come along, which simply would not do for the weekly meetings with the *Ladies of Opportunity,* as they jokingly referred to themselves.

The group, a secret society, kept a betting book much like White's, but which was reserved exclusively for female patrons. That criteria prevented women from becoming indebted to male creditors, which might risk their virtue.

Imagine the *haut ton's* shock should the client list or the nature of the numerous wagers ever be revealed. That must *never* happen. Women who supplemented their income via secret gambling stakes could expect tarnished reputations or ruin should they be found out.

Believable excuses must be contrived to dissuade Aubriella's social butterfly of a sister from accompanying her, and one could not easily deter Minnie. In all fairness to her mother and sister, Aubriella often lost track of time while researching and studying, which, more than anything, accounted for her perpetual tardiness.

Shutting the door, she cast a pensive glance at the ominous pewter sky as she approached the coach's front.

It looks like it may snow.

She gave a joyous internal whoop.

Please. Please. Please snow.

Winter had finally arrived, bringing bitter cold and the possibility of a much-desired snowstorm.

None too soon, either.

Now, if only a foot or two of freezing white fluff would fall and remain on the ground, preventing her family from attending the Templetons' annual Christmastide house party in Westerham. A fortnight of holiday revelry, tedious parlor games, gambling, impromptu recitals, awful skits, and dancing, of course.

All of which Aubriella was wholly inept at, except the wagering.

That particular vice she had become very adept at, indeed.

Her sisters had inherited Mama's fair coloring, curves, beauty, gracefulness, and adoration of all things social. Aubriella took after their father: dark, freckled, thin, and, as Papa was wont to say, "amiably awkward."

Kind but clumsy.

Genial but gauche.

His good-natured maladroitness was endearing.

Hers?

Nothing short of humiliating.

What was worse, the Templetons believed in the adage, *the more the merrier*, and packed the house to the rafters with revelers. That, along with too much mulled wine, hot toddies, abundant champagne, and the gentlemen imbibing in stronger spirits, provided the perfect opportunity for illicit liaisons.

Last year, trying to find a quiet spot to read, she'd stumbled upon no fewer than three amorous couples. That included Jackson Matherfield in the conservatory wrapped in a scandalous embrace with that fast, immoral wanton Francine Willoughby.

Even now, the memory caused Aubriella's cheeks to flame with chagrin, and it was freezing outside. She'd pelted back to her shared bedchamber and pleaded a sick headache for the next four and twenty hours.

Never mind that Aubriella didn't ever suffer from headaches.

But what she'd accidentally witnessed made her head throb with the vengeance of a Highlander's battle drums and proved beyond a doubt that Jackson Matherfield was every bit the rapscallion and rakehell she'd always believed him to be.

Mindful that her friends awaited her, Aubriella slung her satchel strap over her head and adjusted the bag to hang near her waist. The smooth, dark-brown leather concealed so many secrets. Confidences she and the others she was about to meet with had sworn never to reveal.

Keeping one hand firmly against the sealed bag, she peered up at Mosely.

"Pick me up in three hours." Would that give her enough time to ready herself for dinner? "No, you had better make it two."

Mama had invited guests to supper for Emmet's birthday, although for the life of her, Aubriella couldn't remember precisely who would attend and celebrate.

Had Mama told her?

Probably.

Trying to recall, Aubriella pursed her lips. Absorbed with the drawings she'd received from Italy last week, not much else had kept her attention these past few days.

Such magnificent, wondrous, intriguing renderings.

The copies of Leonardo da Vinci's anatomical drawings lay hidden beneath her mattress.

Just thinking about the intricate and detailed works caused her tummy to tumble with giddiness. She *might've* led her parents to believe the sketches were da Vinci's architectural renderings. Architecture wasn't exactly appropriate for a young lady of quality, but it was certainly not as scandalous as the artist's depictions of human dissections.

Aubriella felt little remorse for deceiving her parents.

If women could study medicine, she wouldn't have had to resort to subterfuge. However, until that day came—and she was confident it must—she would unapologetically use whatever means necessary to expand her knowledge of the human body.

Regardless, a formal supper meant Aubriella must dress appropriately. Her usual attire of whatever she wore while studying her specimens would not do, sans her stained laboratory apron, of course.

No, tonight would require a fashionable gown, stays, intricately coiffured hair, jewelry, and perfume. And, of course, her best manners, decorum, and *hours* of insipid small talk. She would struggle to not roll her eyes, yawn, or make a less-than-charitable remark.

So help her God, if anyone mentioned the weather, fashion, or shared a snippet of gossip, she would eschew propriety and suggest a dark, unmentionable cavern where they might shove said exchange.

Since at four and twenty, she was too old to banish to her room, and restricting her social interactions merely brought her relief, her parents had no notion what to do with their middle daughter when she blurted something blush-worthy or indecorous. Which, truth be told, occurred more often than Aubriella cared to admit.

Nevertheless, the skills that came easily to her sisters seemed to have skipped her altogether, along with the ability to dance gracefully, sing in tune, and wield a needle with any skill. Although she'd bet her pin money if women could become surgeons, she'd have managed a needle with considerable aptitude.

Yes, tonight would be another painful reminder of everything Aubriella was and was not. She was plain, solidly on the shelf, and had nothing to look forward to except caring for her parents in their dotage.

And…sneaking around, trying to learn as much about anatomy as possible.

A sparrow amongst doves.

For certain, tonight she would say something stupid, knock over her wineglass, clink her fork or spoon against her plate, or any number of other miniature calamities.

One could wager on it.

Her stomach cramped at the thought, but she forced a smile to her suddenly stiff lips.

"Please tell Widow Waddell hello for me, Mosely."

For the past year, since entering into the clandestine *business venture*, she'd visited Roxina almost weekly. Mosely and the widow had grown quite cozy, and Aubriella hoped he'd propose soon.

"Yes, Miss Penford. I shall." He nodded, giving her a grateful smile, fondness creasing the corners of his kind, nut-brown eyes and wrinkling his weathered face. "I'll just watch until you've entered the house."

He took his duties to deliver Aubriella home unharmed seriously. That meant he was on duty until the door closed behind her. Bracing against the wintry wind buffeting her, she bent her head as she turned and plowed straight into a tall, hard, masculine form.

"Careful there, Miss Penford."

TWO

Still outside Roxina Danforth's House

*B*LAST AND BUNIONS.

Humor deepened the man's baritone, laced with the merest hint of mockery.

Aubriella knew *that* voice.

Bracing herself, she raised her gaze to meet Jackson Matherfield's sinfully beautiful hazel eyes, ringed with dark blue and fringed with ebony lashes.

No man should possess eyes that stunning.

It wasn't right.

If she were a typical female, she might've been jealous or ensnared by their beauty.

Except, she recognized the rakish cynicism glinting in his eyes that most other ladies missed in their mutton-headed ogling. Jackson Matherfield viewed life through sardonic lenses, was seldom serious, and was a *roué* from his charmingly mussed hair to his highly polished Hessians.

Furthermore, this man liked nothing better than to tease and taunt her.

Well, he wouldn't ruffle her today. Mustering every ounce of poise she possessed, Aubriella greeted him cooly. "Mr. Matherfield."

He gave a dramatic sigh as he steadied her, his grip firm yet gentle.

"How many times must I ask you to address me as Jack?" Then the bounder dared to wink as if they were close acquaintances or intimate friends.

"We've known each other most of our lives."

True, but that didn't mean she had forgiven the cad for tormenting her for almost as long.

He'd intended to be annoying but, in truth, he'd done her a great favor.

A smile tried to twist her mouth upward, but Aubriella wrestled her mirth under control.

Jack mustn't think he amused her.

Gads, he was intolerably arrogant as it was. She didn't want to imagine how impossible he would become if he believed she felt anything but disdain toward him. His teasing would increase exponentially.

In truth, the frogs, bugs, snakes, and even the occasional fossil, animal bone, or skull he presented her as a child hadn't frightened her or caused her to cry, shriek, or run away. Instead, she'd examined each one with the diligence of a trained scientist until, at last, he recognized she enjoyed the opportunity to study the creatures that were otherwise off-limits to little girls of genteel breeding.

Not only did Jackson Matherfield live next door to the house she was about to enter, but he was also a bosom chum of her brother, Emmet. Aubriella had known Jack for over fifteen years, and he still vexed her to no end.

He skimmed that gorgeous gaze over her new redingote.

"That berry shade suits you, Aubrie."

Only *he* ever called her that.

Those closest to her addressed her as Elli.

Irritation and impatience stirred in her belly whenever he murmured the name in that seductive purr. It had always been thus between them. They were as different as oil and water or sugar and vinegar, and would never mix well.

"That's not my name, and I'll thank you not to address me as such." Taking the handsome devil to task, when she didn't give a goose's hind end about convention most of the time, screamed irony.

The upward skewing of his nicely—fine, *perfectly*—shaped lips revealed he thought as much, too. Those lips locked on Francine's perfect rosebud of a mouth popped into Aubriella's mind. Any sensual musings she might've indulged in plummeted to her half boots, encasing her rather cold toes.

"Visiting Miss Danforth?" he asked conversationally. The breeze teased the midnight hair, brushing the back of his collar and sent a delicious whiff of tantalizing cologne in her direction.

Must the man smell so blasted divine?

If temptation had an aroma, Jackson Matherfield had doused himself in the essence and was devilishly enticing even to a firmly-on-the-shelf spinster such as herself.

Quirking an eyebrow, she stepped away.

"Obviously." Her droll reply was as dry as desert sand. "Don't you have someplace you need to be? Overseeing one of your establishments?"

He and his brother owned four clubs. He called them restaurants, but she'd heard titillating whispers that the establishments were something much less reputable.

"Wagering on something ridiculous at White's?" *Was he a member of White's?* "Flirting with a debutante?"

Debutantes. Duchesses. Widows. Wallflowers. Elderly dames. Maids…

The man was a consummate charmer, and women flocked to him like ants to spilled honey. He pressed a black-gloved hand to his broad chest, mischief and merriment dancing in his eyes.

Oh, the bounder.

"You wound me, Aubrie, love. You know I *never* flirt with anyone but you."

A snort worthy of a stallion escaped her.

A more susceptible woman might've been taken in by his pretty words and even more alluring, seductive smile. Fortunately, Aubriella lacked most feminine weaknesses and merely found his bedevilment bothersome.

She fashioned a sweetly demure smile in imitation of those she'd seen diamonds of the first water bestow upon gentlemen. A gratified thrill zipped along her pulse when the corners of his eyes flexed the merest bit.

Tit for tat.

Feeling particularly bold and naughty, she leaned toward him, and his nostrils flared.

Hmm. Interesting and unexpected.

"Bollocks to that drivel, *Jack*."

As she stomped up the stairs, his laughter rang in her ears.

"I'm looking forward to continuing this intriguing conversation at supper tonight," he said.

She froze, mid-step.

What?

Supper? Tonight?

One foot resting on the landing, she pivoted halfway around. "I beg your pardon?"

A little warning bell sounded.

Aubriella vaguely recalled Mama mentioning Emmet's friends would attend his birthday celebration.

Blister and blast.

She should've paid more attention. Adjusting her satchel, she sent the driver a swift glance.

Mosley observed the conversation with undisguised amusement. No point in telling him he could leave because he wouldn't budge an inch until she closed the door.

"*Sup-per.*" Did satisfaction gleam in Jack's eyes, the cad? "You know, where people gather, eat, drink, and converse? Sometimes play cards or dance afterward? We've done so numerous times over the years."

"*You* are dining with us tonight?" Aubriella sounded like a simpleton to her own ears.

Of course, Jack was; God save her. It was Emmet's birthday celebration.

Mama had better not seat the scoundrel at the same end of the table as Aubriella, or any wine she spilled would be on purpose.

Straight into his virile lap.

"Indeed. I hope we are seated near each other." Jack lifted the brim of his hat and gave a brief bow. "I'm most curious to learn why you think me flirting with you is drivel."

Refusing to respond to his intentional goading, Aubriella slipped inside, shutting the door a mite firmer than necessary.

"I apologize for my tardiness." Untying her bonnet ribbons, she offered the other women on the club's board a contrite smile. "I do try to be on time."

Waving her apology away, Georgine Thackerly grinned. "We saw *who* detained you, Elli. Jack's such a handsome devil. Too bad he's a rake."

Of course, they had seen, but Aubriella wouldn't discuss the pest next door.

"Come, have a cup of fresh tea and warm yourself," Roxina invited as she poured the brew into a cup with a dab of milk before adding a lump of sugar. "Claire has a wager for us to consider."

Though they guarded the club's existence with extreme care, women covertly spread the word to others who needed to supplement their income and were interested in placing a wager. Truth be told, that criteria meant most females qualified.

The *Ladies of Opportunity* kept a percentage of each bet and, like the women they assisted, could put money aside, keeping them from relying solely on men for financial support. Each potential wager must be unanimously agreed upon and couldn't be cruel or dishonorable in intent, or it wasn't accepted.

Settling onto the outdated beige and black brocade settee, Aubriella nudged aside an equally bedraggled tasseled tapestry pillow before accepting the teacup from Roxina and raising an inquisitive eyebrow toward Claire.

Widowed at eight and twenty, Claire Granlund held the dubious honor of being the eldest of their little troupe of spinsters and misfits.

Claire tilted her golden blonde head, mischief fairly dancing in her whisky brown eyes. "Lady Lovegrove approached me last evening and asked if the society would consider accepting a wager for two hundred pounds."

Georgine gasped, her sapphire blue eyes widening with excitement.

"*Two hundred?*" Her voice pitching high on the last syllable, she glanced in astonishment between Aubriella and Roxina. "Isn't that the largest yet?"

"It is." Expression contemplative, Roxina nodded. "I would guess her ladyship has access to information that makes her certain she shall win. I'll wager that is every cent she has to her name."

"What is the wager, Claire?" Aubriella took a sip of tea, savoring the flavor and warmth. Roxina never skimped on tea, though her circumstances required economizing.

"First," Claire selected a ginger biscuit, holding it midway to her mouth, "she insists on anonymity for the bet."

Aubriella and the others nodded an affirmation. Many women made such requests.

"However, Lady Lovegrove vows Francine Willoughby shall announce her betrothal within a month. She's very likely *enceinte*." Claire whispered the last word as if the walls might overhear the scandalous tidbit, and the wind would carry the tattle throughout London.

Aubriella choked on her tea. *Francine? Pregnant?*

As Francine's paternal aunt, Lady Lovegrove had little liking for the conceited, unkind girl who poked fun at the dowdy, plump widow at every opportunity. One couldn't blame Lady Lovegrove for jumping at the opportunity to profit from her niece's misfortune.

For three Seasons, the promiscuous chit had held out for an earl or duke while *entertaining* a long list of handsome rogues. What man would marry her when he could get her favors for free?

"I wonder who the father is?" Georgine mused, her forefinger on her chin as she squinted at the ceiling in need of fresh paint.

Aubriella suddenly felt quite ill, her stomach toppling over like it had the one time she'd boarded a ship.

Jack? Could he have fathered the child?

"It could be any of a dozen chaps." Claire rolled a delicate shoulder. "We all know Francine hasn't exactly been, *er*, discriminating. 'Tis a wonder she hasn't been *caught* before now."

That was true.

Nevertheless, Aubriella felt a pang of compassion for the foolish girl and much more for the unfortunate child.

"The wager must be about Francine's expedited wedding, not her delicate condition." Aubriella set her cup down, far more composed outwardly than inwardly.

Jack would be miserable with Francine. Perhaps it was what he deserved for dallying with the tart, but a lifetime of unhappiness seemed a cruel fate.

"We are not in the business of ruining lives," Aubriella reiterated.

Sometimes it could not be helped that someone's poor choices led to their destruction, while providing a few coins in the *Ladies of Opportunity's'* purses.

"I pity the unfortunate chap forced to wed that harpy." Unlike Aubriella, Roxina typically had little compassion for anyone who made stupid decisions. "It won't likely be the real father, but a man Willoughby thinks he can blackmail, buy, or manipulate into yielding."

Jack wouldn't easily acquiesce, but then again, he might not be the babe's father.

But if he was, Aubriella had no doubt he would do the honorable thing.

And why that made her want to cry defied explanation.

THREE

Penfords' House, Mayfair—London

HALF EIGHT THAT EVENING

HIDING A TRIUMPHANT SMILE, Jack slid into the seat beside Aubriella. He snapped his serviette open and smoothed it across his black pantaloons. Likely miffed at the seating arrangements, she refused to acknowledge his presence.

She'd come around, eventually.

He knew how to draw her out, though it usually involved her temper flaring. Meanwhile, he would surreptitiously look his fill at the lovely young woman she'd transformed into for dinner.

The candles cast a golden glow on her pretty sable-brown hair and caused the pearls encircling her slender ivory neck and dangling from her shell-like ears to gleam. Her cream muslin gown, with its sea-foam green overskirt and embroidered flowers at the hem and around the sleeves, enhanced the fern-green in her hazel eyes.

Unlike her sisters, Aubriella would never be considered a beauty by society's limited and warped standards. Jessamine and Lenora were lovely—roses or peonies in full bloom. But tall and slender, Aubriella was a delphinium or gladiolus.

He hid a grin behind his wineglass.

She would loathe the comparison.

Though most women adored flowers, she'd always preferred medicinal plants, herbs, or even weeds. Yes, Aubriella Kendra Larkspur Penford was remarkably unique.

Jack's interest in her wasn't romantic.

After all, she was his good friend's sister, and he'd known Aubriella for so long that they were practically family. He supposed his fascination with her stemmed from him appreciating a challenge, and she was the most provoking woman he'd ever met. Her disdain and dislike of him had puzzled him for years, and try as he might, he couldn't recall what he'd done to earn her disfavor.

He glanced across the table to where his and Emmet Penford's longtime friend, Shelby Tellinger, regarded Roxina Danforth with barely concealed mockery. Roxina's brother, Mitchel, seated at Aubriella's right, was Tellinger's best friend.

It was a peculiar coupling as Tellinger was an upright chap and several years younger, though a tad temperamental and serious. On the other hand, Mitchel Danforth was a wastrel and fop, and those were his good qualities.

He treated his sister abominably, and she openly held in contempt anyone who called themselves Mitchel's friends. Thus, she and Tellinger were constantly at odds.

In truth, they were rather like Jack and Aubriella, although for entirely different reasons.

"That gown is very becoming." Jack sipped his wine, awaiting Aubriella's response.

None came.

So, she meant to play that game, did she?

Give him the silent treatment?

Hadn't she learned by now he knew exactly how to maneuver past her bastions?

Servants cleared the artichoke soup, replacing it with fish seasoned with fennel and mint. The Penfords, like the others seated at the table, weren't aristocrats, though some present had aristocratic relatives, such as himself. These were genteel people, hovering on the fringes of *le beau monde* and considered vulgar by the *haut ton* because they earned a living.

"Are you going to ignore me the entire evening?" Jack whispered near Aubriella's ear, inhaling her subtle perfume—light and citrusy with a hint of jasmine. She'd gone all out for her brother's birthday, which showed how much she adored Emmet.

She stiffened so slightly that no one else noticed and pasted a false smile on her face.

"I'm *not* ignoring you."

Bugger me if she isn't.

"You are, Aubrie, but I'm at a loss as to why."

A moment later, Jack's thigh burned with sharp pain.

She'd pinched him.

The vixen actually pinched him.

"My name is not Aubrie."

A chuckle throttled up his throat.

He swept his gaze across the table.

Georgine Thackerly, another of Aubriella's good friends, watched him, three neat lines furrowing her forehead. Her astute gaze traveled back and forth between him and Aubriella before, with a small indefinable smile, she inclined her head to listen to something Robyn Fitzlloyd said.

Jack shifted his attention back to Aubriella.

That had been the case more and more this past year or so.

Whenever she was near, he couldn't seem to pull his focus away. Maybe it was because he felt sorry for her. She'd wanted to become a physician or a surgeon, but women were forbidden in the profession.

She was practically invisible to her parents, and with diamond-of-the-first-water sisters who always drew the lion's share of attention, she'd resigned herself to spinsterhood and studying her science specimens.

What a colossal waste of womanhood and wit.

Head tilted, Aubriella listened to Mitchel Danforth ramble on. At least she pretended to listen. From the faraway look in her eyes, her thoughts were elsewhere.

Jack couldn't fault her for her inattentiveness.

Danforth, the long-winded sot, could blather on for ages without saying a dashed thing remotely intelligent or interesting. Add his boasting and self-important prattling to the one-sided conversation, and even the staunchest adherer to decorum's mind would've wandered.

Why had the Penfords invited that rotter to Emmet's birthday celebration?

Jack glanced up and down both sides of the table.

Likely to even out the males and females.

Heaven forbid that there be one man or one woman too many.

The stars might fall from the sky, or the tides cease to turn.

In all, fourteen people sat at the table.

The Penfords, their eldest daughter Lenora and her husband, Stephen Langford, accounted for seven. The Danforths, Georgine Thackerly, and Jack made eleven. Friends of Jack's and Emmet's, Shelby Tellinger and his cousins Robyn and Matilda Fitzlloyd, completed the guests.

How often had these same people, sans Mitchel Danforth, gathered over the years?

Too many to count, and in truth, they were more like family than Jack's kin, except for his younger brother, who couldn't attend tonight because Duncan was away on business.

Aubriella lifted her attention from the fish Danforth had unceremoniously plopped upon her plate moments before and caught Jack staring at her. Instead of averting his gaze, he winked, and her hazel-green eyes widened the merest bit before she presented her profile again.

Sighing inwardly at the polite coolness she generally directed toward him, Jack leveled Danforth a contemplative glance.

The man was an ignorant buffoon.

Though acceptable for a gentleman to serve the ladies nearest him, said gentleman might inquire whether the lady desired fish. Anyone who knew Aubriella at all knew she didn't eat fish.

It gave her hives.

So did strawberries.

Having known her since she was a curious, tousle-haired nine-year-old with eyes too large for her thin face, Jack knew those and a hundred other inconsequential details about her.

Danforth's fawning attention raised Jack's hackles.

Since when had the libertine shown an interest in Aubriella?

Was he at home when she visited Roxina?

It was none of Jack's business, but the notion rankled, particularly given Danforth's unsavory reputation. Maybe he ought to have a private word with Emmet or Mr. Penford regarding the matter.

Not that independent and fiery Aubriella would listen to her brother or father.

"What are you currently studying?" Jack speared a piece of flaky fish. "I believe Emmet mentioned something about da Vinci's drawings?"

The most intelligent woman Jack had ever met, Aubriella eyed him as if she wasn't sure if he jested or was serious. "Yes, I recently acquired a few copies. They are quite interesting."

Her standoffish demeanor did nothing to dissuade him.

"I'd love to see them." He truly would.

Da Vinci was a genius, his work inspiring.

Aubriella's face drained of color before she recovered and cleared her throat. "I'm sure they'd bore you."

Eyes slightly narrowed, Jack regarded her. Red apples had formed on her cheeks, waxen but seconds before. If he had to guess, he'd suspect she was nervous and hiding something.

Just what were the drawings she'd attained?

"I'd wager one of my restaurants that you're not studying his inventions." He cocked an eyebrow in challenge.

She shook her head, the curls left to frame her face, swaying with the motion. "No, they're—"

"Will you and your brother join us at the Templetons' again this year, Jack?" Mrs. Penford asked with her fork poised halfway to her mouth, thereby saving Aubriella from answering.

From beneath his lashes, Jack cast her a swift glance.

Hand halfway to her wineglass, she froze and turned those magnificent eyes upon him.

She silently asked, *"Will you?"*

Until this moment, he'd been undecided. He nodded. "If Duncan and I can get away, we shall, Mrs. Penford."

Did Aubriella's mouth turn downward the merest bit?

Why was she so averse to him?

Jack took a deep sip of wine, savoring the flavor before the liquid slid down his throat.

Since she turned fourteen or fifteen, she'd been far more reserved than she had as a child when he'd brought her many interesting things to examine. But this past year, she'd become positively frigid in his presence. It was as if he'd offended her, but he didn't know how.

"Robyn and I are attending as well." Miss Fitzlloyd smiled at her older brother, and he kicked his mouth upward into an affectionate grin.

"As if you gave me any choice, minx. She's been talking about naught else for weeks now." He dabbed his mouth with his napkin and glanced around the table. "Does anyone else intend to make the trip?"

Westerham lay just over twenty miles away.

Like Jack, many of the other guests tonight were parentless, and the kindhearted Templetons had begun inviting the orphans for holidays years ago. Mrs. Templeton was Mrs. Penford's bosom girlhood friend and cousin, so the families usually spent the holiday together.

"I hope it snows from now until next week." Aubriella's heated statement, mumbled beneath her breath, yanked Jack's attention back to her. She stared at her plate, an aura of defeat about her.

"Why?" He cut a piece of mackerel. "Don't you want to attend the Templetons' house party?"

"No. I. Do. not." She snapped each clipped syllable under her breath.

"Why not?" Jack believed she enjoyed the annual gathering, though he'd usually been too busy celebrating and making merry to notice whether Aubriella did or didn't. Guilt kicked him in the ribs.

She licked her lower lip and, after casting a swift glance toward her mother, leaned toward him. Once more, her fragrance tickled his senses.

"You know I'm hopeless at those sorts of gatherings, Jack. I stick out like a lame goose among graceful swans. I never know what to say or do and inevitably embarrass myself."

Trying not to appear too smug because she'd addressed him by his given name and because she'd confided in him, Jack gave the back of her hand a fleeting, comforting touch even as his ribs cramped with compassion.

He hated how she disparaged herself.

"What if I promise to stay by your side the entire time?" The words formed of their own volition before passing through his mind. Now he'd have to make sure he attended.

"Surely, not the *entire* time." Mirth twinkled in Aubriella's eyes. She rarely indulged in witticisms, but he took her meaning.

"Yes. Quite," Jack agreed with an answering upward sweep of his mouth.

A servant interrupted to refill their wine glasses, and Jack continued once the footman had stepped away. "I meant that I shan't leave you alone during any planned events or public gatherings. You can depend on me to help you through every situation."

Wonder and suspicion shadowed her mesmerizing hazel eyes. "Why would you do that?"

Why, indeed?

"Because that's what friends do." Jack had never had female friends, so he wasn't certain that was entirely true.

Oh, he flirted and bantered incessantly.

What harm was there in making a woman feel pretty or appreciated?

He'd even pried an ardent female or several off his person, but the truth was, Jack was a virgin. A wholly unpopular state amongst his randy peers and a secret no one but his brother knew, and he meant to keep it that way.

A small furrow appeared on Aubriella's forehead as she skated her glance over his face.

Laughter rang out from the head of the table, momentarily gaining Jack's attention.

"*Friends.*" She murmured the word as if she had tasted something foreign for the first time. "You and me... *friends.*"

"Is that such a hard prospect to consider?" he asked.

Once more, servants collected their plates, forcing him to wait as they placed the wild game and meats on the pristine linen. Across the table, Robyn Fitzlloyd caught his eye and raised a hawkish eyebrow in silent question when he swung his focus to Danforth.

Ah, he also wondered why the bounder dined with them.

Hopefully, Danforth wouldn't attend the house party. His presence was as unwelcome as maggots and would surely put a damper on the festivities as well as put every woman under sixty at risk of ruin.

"It won't inconvenience you?" Aubriella's softly spoken question brought Jack back to the present. "Keep you from other more exciting and invigorating—ah—activities?"

Jack almost choked on his mouthful.

Surely she didn't imply…?

He raised his shoulder an inch in response. "No, it's not an inconvenience."

Jack's pulse accelerated at the prospect of spending amiable time with Aubriella without conflict, barbed and cutting ripostes, and darkling looks. It would also spare him the unwanted and unsolicited attention of devious vixens such as Francine Willoughby and her ilk.

"I should count it a great honor, Aubrie." Giving her a naughty grin, he wiggled his eyebrows. "Imagine the tongue wagging it will cause. The speculation."

As he'd expected, Aubriella rolled her eyes ceilingward and bent her full mouth into a droll smile. "I don't relish being the object of gossip, and you shouldn't either, though I'm certain you're quite accustomed to it."

Jack canted his head. There was an unspoken message in her words, but bugger him if he had any idea what it was. "I try to refrain from activities that give chinwags fuel for fodder."

"*Hmph.*" Distinct disbelief weighted Aubriella's unladylike grunt.

"You don't believe me, Aubrie."

It was a statement, not a question.

Why did she doubt him?

Had she heard rumors?

Was that what caused her coolness?

"Have you heard something I should know, Aubrie?"

Once more, she looked positively ill but shook her dark head, causing her earrings to swing back and forth. Nevertheless, when she met his eyes, distrust and uncertainty lingered in the depths of hers, the color of a forest at twilight.

She filled her lungs, causing her bosom to swell temptingly, then released the air in a rush. "Oh, very well. Though I'm positive I shall regret the impulse, I accept your offer."

"Excellent." Jack barely suppressed a jubilant grin. "And I promise you *shan't* regret it." He had every intention of assuring Aubriella had nothing to repine upon and much to celebrate for trusting him.

This was his one chance to prove himself to her, and by thunder, he'd not muck it up.

FOUR

Stockworth Manor—Templetons' estate,
Westerham, England

19 December 1818 – Breakfast

GOD HAD NOT DUMPED several feet of snow on London and answered Aubriella's fervent prayers that she might be spared the Templetons' Christmas house party. The day after Emmet's birthday dinner, she'd awoken to a mere dusting, as disappointingly light as confectioners' sugar sprinkled on almond cake.

Regardless, the holiday gathering mightn't be a complete loss. With just over thirty people in attendance, half of which were women, there could be multiple opportunities for placing discreet wagers and bets.

Taking a sip of cocoa, she surreptitiously swept her gaze around the Templetons' expensive but tastefully decorated dining room. Only a few of the more intrepid guests had arisen early and ventured below to break their fasts.

Most of the ladies—*and potential clients*—either remained snuggly asleep or had ordered trays in their chambers like Mama usually did. Jessamine never rose a minute before ten, and Papa had probably already ridden out with the other men for an early morning constitutional.

At Mama's insistence, Aubriella had only packed her newest gowns, outerwear, and slippers. She'd been forbidden to wear her faded work frocks and apron.

Dear Mama still held an unrealistic hope that Aubriella might find herself a suitable husband. It escaped her what gentleman her mother thought would attend the Templetons' party that Aubriella didn't already know and would show an interest in her.

For the most part, men looked past her as one did an urn in the foyer or a statue in the garden. One knew something was there, but the object wasn't riveting or intriguing enough to garner one's full attention.

She was unremarkable.

Ordinary.

And above all, a realist.

It was as unlikely as jewels falling from the sky, for an unattached man Aubriella would find striking to find her attractive, too.

"You cannot be seen in those rags, my dear. What man would consider you if you don't take care with your appearance?" Mama had patted her cheek and given her an indulgent smile. "You might not have mine and your sisters' fair coloring, Elli, but you are not unattractive."

Mama had intended to encourage Aubriella, but the backhanded compliment fell short of the mark. Mama loved her. Aubriella didn't doubt her affection. But the truth was, her mother didn't understand her middle daughter.

Mama wished to talk of fashion and soirees and to share gossip, recipes, and scandal. All of which Aubriella had no interest in. Should her parents ever learn of the outrageous da Vinci drawings hidden in her bedchamber…

A shiver tripped across her shoulders.

Lord, Aubriella didn't want to consider what her mild-mannered parents would do. Even they drew boundaries at what was acceptable and what was not, and she'd crossed those marks long before now.

When she'd dressed as a man and sneaked into the biology laboratory at university seven years ago, her parents had expressed their disappointment in the calmest tones. They'd sent her to her prissy spinster aunt's outside of London for the summer.

They'd undoubtedly prayed Aunt Astrid's prim, proper, and boring-as-Hades decorum would rub off on Aubriella.

It had not.

After Aubriella volunteered to assist the local doctor in setting an unfortunate lad's badly broken leg—really, the blood didn't make her the least faint, but poor Aunt Astrid *had* swooned—she'd been sent home as incorrigible.

However, in an odd and unforeseen twist, Aunt Astrid had bequeathed Aubriella her small house. Possibly because her aunt believed her irredeemable, unmarriable niece might find herself in need of a home someday.

If it hadn't been for Jackson Matherfield, Aubriella felt certain her subterfuge would've worked—another reason to dislike the scoundrel.

How was she to know he was in that class?

Fate must, indeed, have something against her.

Despite what she believed to be a remarkably good disguise, he'd recognized her immediately. She still hadn't forgiven him, though instead of revealing her to the professor and other students, he had let her escape with her reputation intact.

He had, however, told her parents, the rotter.

Had he wanted to, he might've ruined her that day.

Women were strictly prohibited from such courses.

Another stupid rule made by men.

Since marrying had never been at the forefront of Aubriella's desires, her disappointment in her continued spinsterhood was less significant than Mama's discontent.

To appease her mother, Aubriella wore a long-sleeved navy-blue velvet day gown trimmed in black today. The pretty gown complemented her coloring and lithe figure, bolstering her confidence by a small degree. Nevertheless, she felt as out of place as a dull river rock among glittering, polished gems.

This morning, Roxina sat beside Aubriella with Matilda Fitzlloyd across from them. Aubriella hadn't met the two couples babbling away like magpies at the foot of the table, nor the pair of indolent gentlemen halfway down the large rectangle and currently engaged in low conversation with Emmet and Quinten Honeybrook.

No doubt, Mama and Mabel Templeton would play matchmaker and devise a scheme or several to throw Aubriella into the company of the newcomers. She couldn't help but suspect the cousins had plotted together toward that very end.

Three days ago, Aubriella's family had rumbled up the circular drive to the Templetons' grand estate. As always, they were the first guests to arrive so that Mama and Cousin Mabel might enjoy a short, intimate visit before the other invitees descended upon the estate.

At least Aubriella had Jack's promise that he'd help her through the next two weeks.

If he came.

How peculiar that she anticipated seeing him when she normally went out of her way to avoid him. His presence was less objectionable than making a fool of herself—that was what she'd been telling herself since she'd impulsively accepted his offer.

So far, he and his brother remained absent, and something between disappointment and lack of surprise sat heavy and dull in Aubriella's belly. As she'd descended the stairs for breakfast, she told herself she didn't need him to manage the festivities. After all, she'd endured these annual gatherings her entire life. Another fortnight shouldn't be so unbearable.

Even as she tried to convince herself, doubts lingered.

Why this year should be different, she didn't know.

If only Jack hadn't raised her hopes that she might be spared indignity and humiliation during this holiday season.

So stupid of her to have trusted him.

Although, to be fair, he had said he'd attend if he could get away from his business obligations. Aubriella imagined there must be many responsibilities with four successful ventures. Regardless, she shouldn't have counted on him, and annoyance at herself for doing so chaffed her pride.

Aubriella squared her shoulders as she picked up a triangle of toast.

She'd simply do as she'd always done at these assemblies.

Find an out-of-the-way spot to retreat to whenever possible, and when she couldn't escape, paint a benign expression on her face and pretend she didn't care that she was a dismal failure. She'd laugh at her maladroitness with the others, and no one but her dearest friends or family would know how keenly she suffered.

"Do you suppose they are without family, and Mrs. Templeton has taken them beneath her wing?" Roxina nudged her chin toward the babbling foursome. "If she keeps it up, we'll be four to a chamber."

As it was, everyone shared their chamber with at least one person and, in some cases, with two others.

Aubriella didn't mind.

At Blenstock & Handcastle Academy for Young Ladies, Aubriella, Matilda, Roxina, and Georgine had shared a bedchamber. Nonetheless, an orphan herself, Mabel Templeton's soft heart knew no bounds, and she'd continue to take in waifs as long as her house could hold them.

Aubriella shrugged as she chewed her toast and then swallowed. "More than likely, though I do not know where she finds them since she rarely visits Town."

"They're like stray cats." Matilda gave a sage nod. "Start feeding one and soon a dozen will expect a meal."

She just might be correct.

Roxina gave a cursory glance around the dining room. "Do you suppose the Templetons invited the Willoughbys? I haven't seen Lord Willoughby or Francine, though I confess, I'm relieved to have been spared their foul company."

Aubriella's stomach soured, curdling the hot chocolate.

She'd wondered that very thing, but refrained from inquiring. And, truth be told, she had convinced herself that if Francine didn't come this year, that meant Jack was off the matrimonial hook.

Most of the guests had arrived and settled into their respective bedchambers. Surely if Francine were in the family way, she'd be intent on finding a husband, even if the Willoughbys were George Templeton's relations.

Francine's absence also bespoke Jack's innocence, and Aubriella breathed a trifle easier. Though why she should fret about the consequences of his actions wasn't the least logical.

The house party activities officially began with archery and sketching this morning, decorating greenery to festoon the mansion this afternoon, and gambling and charades this evening.

A schedule chock full of daily activities culminated in a grand ball on Christmas Eve where Aubriella was sure to forget a step or trod upon her partners' feet—*if* anyone partnered her.

Last year, only Papa, Emmet, and Lenora's husband, Stephen Langford, had done so, much to Aubriella's chagrin. This year, she'd intended to find a cozy alcove to read in until supper was served at midnight.

It did rather wear on one's pride being relegated to the status of an undesirable.

The exuberant quartet burst into laughter, and several guests, including Aubriella, glanced in their direction. Oblivious to the attention they'd drawn, they rose from the table and departed the dining room; the women arm in arm and the gentlemen with their heads together.

Were they related?

"I must work on my charades clue." Matilda rested her elbow on the table, her chin on her fist. "I don't want to make it too easy."

For variety, Mabel insisted each guest create at least one clue per game.

Aubriella loathed charades.

All that ridiculous posturing and gesturing, not to mention the preposterous clues.

How did one contrive such absurd rhyming riddles and conundrums?

For certain, she'd never been able to compose anything remotely clever and had long since stopped trying. Jessamine had written a riddle for Aubriella's topics for the past three years, and they'd been ghastly.

Hives. Sleepwalking. Gout.

She still shuddered at the memories.

Hopeless at everything but sketching, Aubriella had already decided to hide away in the library's loft. Over the years, she'd learned her presence was rarely missed. Except sometimes by her family and dearest friends, who understood her desire to remain elusive.

That unfortunate truth ought to sting more than it did, but always pragmatic, she refused to sulk or pout over what she couldn't control.

She had hoped that with Jack's help, this yuletide might be different. That she might look forward to the caroling, games, decorations, stirring the Christmas pudding, and mayhap a sleigh ride.

Foolish ninny. Goose.

A tiny sigh escaped her, earning her a sharp look from Roxina, who knew her better than any other living soul since their days in finishing school together.

"Are you quite well, Aubriella?" Roxina asked. "You seem a trifle preoccupied."

"Fit as a fiddle. Content as a cat." Aubriella fashioned what she hoped was a bright smile. "Bright as a button. Happy as a hare."

Mayhap too much?

Sable eyebrows high on her forehead, Roxina snorted in disbelief.

Yes, definitely too much.

Aubriella tempered her expression and tone to a more believable mien. "And looking forward to today's activities."

Liar.

"Now I know you're either ailing or touched in the head." Suspicion narrowed Roxina's chestnut-brown eyes. "I'd wager you'd rather eat slugs and grubs than participate in today's events. Or the activities scheduled for the entire fortnight."

"You're wrong, Roxina, and you'd lose that bet." Aubriella widened her smile to such a degree her face might crack. "I've determined to enjoy myself this year."

She leaned near her friend. "We might even add a few wagers to our books. There's always something worth betting on at an extended house party."

Matilda and Roxina exchanged a she's-blathering-like-a-madwoman glance.

"And what makes *this* year different?" Skepticism riddled Roxina's question.

But then again, Roxina was the most sardonic woman Aubriella had ever known. She trusted few women and men not at all.

That was her brother's doing as well.

"May I join you?"

Glancing over her shoulder, Aubriella barely suppressed her astonished gasp.

Jack.

FIVE

The dining room

*A DOZEN **fluttery heartbeats later***

Jack had come.

And what was more, he'd sought Aubriella out first thing this morning. Two weeks ago, his attention would've infuriated her, but today?

Today, he'd become her rescuer.

Her savior.

Her hero.

Unfamiliar giddiness replaced the leaden weight in her tummy.

Because the truth of it was, she *did* mind being a maladroit laughingstock and the last person grudgingly chosen for games. She *did* notice the pitying glances and quickly shushed whispers about her ineptness.

Sometimes, not so hushed judgmental gasps, too.

For instance, when Aubriella sent the pall mall ball sailing across the lawn, the wooden sphere had smacked

Lord Bradrawy in his prominent nose, bloodying the appendage. And when someone had bumped her during her turn at Snapdragon, Aubriella had tipped the bowl of flaming raisins and almonds over.

She still wasn't positive Francine Willoughby hadn't shoved her on purpose.

No one, not even a woman dedicated to science and logic, enjoyed constantly being the brunt of others' jokes. If success this yuletide meant swallowing her pride and accepting her nemesis's help, then Aubriella would choke on her blasted pride.

Especially, if said adversary was dastardly handsome and suave in a striking charcoal-gray coat, irritatingly skilled at all that she was not, and a favorite among the usual guests.

Just this once, Aubriella wanted to fit in.

Now that Jack was here, and if he fulfilled his promise, mayhap this yuletide gathering would be bearable, if not enjoyable, after all.

Jack set a full plate on the table before pulling out the vacant chair to her left. Without waiting for her reply, he sank his tall, lean form onto the green velvet cushion. Freshly shaved, his raven hair still slightly damp, and cologne wafting from his much too masculine form, he appeared at ease.

He always had.

She couldn't recall a time when he'd been anything but nonchalant. Not indolent, just entirely at ease with himself. Something Aubriella still struggled with because she didn't meet her family's or society's expectations.

How the devil did Jack manage such insouciance?

As if he neither noticed nor gave a fig what others thought of him.

In truth, he probably didn't.

From down the table, Emmet nodded a greeting,

which Jack returned with a half-smile and a jaunty wave. Quentin Honeybrook also dipped his chin in a brief greeting.

"Duncan will be along shortly." After snapping his napkin open, Jack placed the linen across his lap. Aubriella tried not to notice how well his muscled thighs filled his buff-colored pantaloons. "We arrived well past midnight, and he was reluctant to leave his mattress this morn."

"Good morning, Mr. Matherfield." Matilda bobbed her head, the unruly riot of bright red curls held in place by a green ribbon wrapped around her head and tied beneath her chignon, threatening to spring loose at the motion. "We weren't certain you'd be able to tear yourself away from London."

"I have excellent managers, Miss Fitzlloyd, who I trust implicitly." Jack veered his gaze toward Roxina. "Miss Danforth. No brother?"

He didn't seem disappointed by Mitchel Danforth's absence.

No one did.

Not even Roxina.

Roxina sat back in her tufted chair and crossed her arms across her remade gown. A gesture Aubriella had learned years ago was as much a protective measure as a deterrent. "No. My brother had other plans for the holiday."

Plans which never included Roxina, and that was why she always came with the Penfords. It was that or spend the holiday alone since her parents died when she was thirteen.

A light eater content with toast and cocoa, Aubriella eyed Jack's overflowing plate. "Hungry this morning, Mr. Matherfield?"

"Ravenous." He speared a sausage with his fork and

grinned before taking a generous bite. He swallowed and took a sip of black coffee.

"So, what are we undertaking this morning, Aubrie?"

Jack applied himself to his breakfast with admirable gusto.

So happy and relieved he'd actually come, Aubriella didn't scold him for addressing her so informally in front of her friends. Nor did she give Roxina and Matilda the gimlet eye for the smug smiles they exchanged.

"It's either archery or sketching this morning." Aubriella wrapped her palm around the still-warm cup.

He patted his mouth—*such a nicely shaped mouth for a man.* "I presume you'd prefer sketching?"

Her one strength.

A Corinthian, he'd opt for archery, of course.

A wry half-smile twisted her mouth upward. "As my previous attempts at archery resulted in me nearly impaling a footman and Lady Brummelstroot's beloved poodle, your presumption is correct."

It had taken an hour to calm Lady Brummelstroot. To this day, she glowered at Aubriella whenever their paths crossed, which, thank goodness, wasn't often.

"Elli is truly awful at archery." Matilda sent Aubriella an apologetic glance.

"*Thank you,* Tillie." Aubriella couldn't quite keep the sarcasm from her tone.

It was true, but Matilda needn't expound upon Aubriella's lack of prowess. On the other hand, Matilda could send an arrow to the center of the target with seemingly little effort.

"Dearest, you know I mean no offense." Matilda waved at Georgine as she entered. "Excuse me, please. Georgine wanted to speak with me this morning."

Roxina pushed her chair back and rose. Smoothing a

long-fingered hand down her out-of-fashion emerald green gown, she scooted her gaze from person to person.

"I promised Mrs. Templeton I'd help with the skit preparations." She wrinkled her pert nose. "This year, it's about the angels visiting the shepherd in their fields."

Cousin Mabel believed her skits quite clever.

Her guests did not share her enthusiasm.

Roxina cast an exasperated glance upward. "Pray tell me how I am to recruit a cast for that?" She pinned Jack with a direct look. "I'm sure I can count on you to play the part of a shepherd?"

"Indeed." He flashed her one of his disarming grins. "Unless you need an archangel?"

"*Hmm*, I'll consider it." She turned her attention to Aubriella. "I'll need you to be part of the angelic chorus."

Oh, no.

"Zina, I don't think—" Before Aubriella could finish refusing, Jack accepted on her behalf.

"Aubrie would love to."

The bothersome scoundrel knows I cannot sing.

"Excellent." After a satisfied nod, Roxina glided across the room, attracting more than one interested male's gaze. She ignored them.

"Why did you do that?" Aubriella poked Jack's arm and hissed, "You know I cannot sing."

"I'll be right there, and I *can* sing. Just follow me." He winked, and her pulse fluttered.

"Easier said than done," Aubriella muttered, still confused at the strange physical response he'd invoked.

"My dear Aubrie, when will you learn to trust me?"

His eyes darkened to sooty hazel blue, then he touched the back of her hand as he had done at dinner the other night. Such an innocent gesture, so why did tingles zip up her arm?

Aubriella slanted her head.

"Honestly? I have spent so long distrusting you, Jack, that I find it hard to lower my ramparts."

Rather than mock her as was his wont, he gave a slow nod, his expression grave. "Let's declare a truce for the house party. I shan't tease you, and you won't shut me out."

It sounded so simple. Innocent. And logical, given he'd promised to help her.

So why did alarm bells toll in the back of her mind?

Regardless, what choice did Aubriella have?

"Agreed." She pointed her forefinger and shook it. "But only for the house party's duration, Jack. I cannot promise more."

"That's all the time I need." His grin was positively feline as he dove into his breakfast once more.

What the devil did he mean by that?

It's all the time he needs.

For what?

SIX

Stockworth Manor

*AFTER SUPPER **that evening***

"LET'S go through to the ladies, gentlemen." George Templeton rose, his rotund belly bumping the table and rattling a few crystal tumblers. "My missus has delightful entertainment planned for the evening."

Finally.

Jack had promised not to leave Aubriella's side, but he couldn't conceive of an excuse for not partaking in spirits and cigars with the men and joining the women instead.

Wouldn't that cause the rumor mills to spin?

Normally, the hour after supper passed quickly with discussions about politics, horses, trade, and ribald jokes. However, aware Aubriella fended for herself, he'd checked his timepiece with increasing impatience every few minutes.

Twice, he'd glanced up to see Baron Spencer

Willoughby observing him with a strange expression on his dissipated countenance. Though kin to George Templeton—*second or third cousins?*—Jack had never cared for the Willoughbys. Not only did they put on haughty airs and treat those without a title like underlings, but they were also a slimy lot.

Jack couldn't count the times Francine, as wanton as a dockside harlot, had invited him to bed her these past three years. Last December, she'd followed him to the conservatory, and it had been all he could do to pry her off him. This year, he'd ensure he was occupied and was never alone with her, and Aubriella provided that insurance.

Ugly rumors also circulated that old man Willoughby possessed an unnatural appetite for young boys. It was a wonder anyone included them in their social circles, but then all manner of excuses were made for wealthy aristocrats' deplorable behavior.

Jack wasted no time departing the dining room. Eager to keep his promise to Aubriella that he'd stay by her side, he'd made it halfway down the corridor when Lord Willoughby waylaid him.

"I would have a word with you, Matherfield."

"*Now?*" Jack stepped aside to permit the other gentlemen to pass. "Can it not wait?"

"No. It cannot." Willoughby shook his head, his fleshy jowls jiggling back and forth like a hound on the hunt. Once the last man had turned the corner and was out of earshot, Willoughby puffed out his substantial chest. "Francine is pregnant. You shall marry her within a fortnight."

Jack barely refrained from putting a finger in his ears to make sure he'd heard Lord Willoughby correctly. "I beg your pardon?"

Surely he had misheard.

"You and Francine shall be wed," Willoughby announced as if discussing what jam to smear on his scone.

"Whether your daughter is with child is not my concern. I have never been intimate with her." *Or any other female, for that matter.* "She's shared her favors far and wide. I sincerely doubt *she* knows who the father is."

Willoughby's face turned an astonishing shade of purplish-red.

"Be that as it may," he sputtered in outraged offense, "she has chosen *you*."

Jack leaned against the wall, arms folded, a ruse against the feral urge to seize Willoughby by his fat throat and shake him to within an inch of his miserable life.

"And Francine always gets what she wants?" Jack's silky timbre would've alerted a man smarter than Lord Willoughby. Shaking his head, Jack bared his teeth, no longer caring to act the part of a gentleman. "She won't have her way this time. I shall not marry the chit. Ever."

His face contorting in fury, Willoughby stomped forward. Shaking with ire, he lifted a fisted hand. "I can ruin you, Matherfield."

"You can try." Jack straightened, looking down at the older man and letting the rage tunneling through his veins manifest in his gravelly voice. "But I can produce at *least* a half dozen men—some in this very house, in truth—who haven't a qualm about revealing they've bedded your daughter."

"You… you wouldn't dare." Willoughby had worked himself into such a state that spittle formed on the side of his mouth. "No gentleman would denounce a lady so cravenly."

"Despite your title, Willoughby, your daughter is *no* lady."

Willoughby opened and shut his mouth several times, only managing to emit strangled, gurgling noises.

Jack hadn't finished taking the pompous man down several pegs. "All of London is aware of her loose morals." He leaned forward. "Do you know she's called *Fickle Francine?*"

And a few other crude terms Jack refused to let pass his lips.

Willoughby made a choking-growling sound deep in his throat and raised his hand as if to strike Jack.

"I would not, Willoughby, because as you've said, I'm no gentleman. I shan't hesitate to lay you out like a rug despite the difference in our ages."

Jack shook his head and stepped around the infuriated older man who looked on the verge of an apoplexy.

"I suggest you take her back to London and find a doddering old fool who doesn't mind claiming another man's child. I'm sure if the price is sufficient, you'll have more than one offer." He drove home the final nail. "But you'd better make haste. You'll not be able to hide her condition indefinitely."

Jack presented his back, and seething with black rage, strode down the corridor.

Francine, the little tramp, thought she'd entrap him?

Snap her manicured fingers, and Papa would make everything right?

Willoughby erroneously believed he could use his position to blackmail Jack.

Another feral snarl contorted his mouth before he wrestled it under control.

That showed how little either he or his daughter knew him.

Jack hadn't become the success he had by allowing others to manipulate or take advantage of him. And by damn, no high-born trollop with the morals of an alley cat would ever become Mrs. Jackson Matherfield.

Outside the drawing room, he closed his eyes and filled his lungs with calming air. Storming into the room would only stir the pot. No one need know what had transpired between him and Willoughby unless the sod was an imbecile and blathered about the matter.

"There you are." Duncan, wearing his perpetual grin, his dark blue eyes twinkling, emerged from the card room. At once, his genial expression faded.

"What has happened, Jack?" He glanced down the corridor toward the dining room. "I saw Willoughby corner you but thought nothing of it."

Jack cupped his tense neck where several stones seemed to have taken up residence. "He thought he could force me to wed his pregnant daughter, and I refused. Most adamantly."

Duncan whistled as he slowly shook his dark head. "That explains why Miss Willoughby keeps flitting from room to room as if looking for someone. Thrice, she asked me if I knew where you were. Given I know how much you dislike her, I should've suspected something untoward was afoot."

"Would you be a good chap and make sure Willoughby is preparing to depart this evening?" Jack slapped his brother's shoulder. "I'm reluctant to divulge his attempt at blackmail to our hosts and put a damper on the festivities." Especially since he'd promised Aubriella that she would enjoy herself this year. "But if he refuses to take his daughter and make for London straightaway, I shall."

"I'd be happy to send the bounder on his way." Thunder in his eyes and outrage causing a muscle in his jaw to tick, Duncan swore softly. "I never liked either of them. Good riddance to bad rubbish, I say. I'll find you when they've left."

After watching his brother until he disappeared from sight and was once more in control of his emotions, Jack ambled into the tastefully decorated drawing room. Though wealthy, the Templetons didn't feel the need to brandish their prosperity. He snatched two flutes from a passing servant's tray and then searched the room.

Thank God Francine wasn't present, but Aubriella was.

Holding the glasses of sparkling wine, Jack wended through the guests toward Aubriella, perched like a nervous cat at the end of a settee. Surrounded by a half dozen chattering women, she appeared regal in her champagne and ecru lace gown. Only the tautness of her delicate jaw and the occasional flick of her tongue over her lower lip betrayed her unease.

When had she become so accomplished at hiding her feelings?

"Mr. Matherfield." Mabel motioned him forward with a wave of her plump, be-ringed hand. "My husband tells me you are considering investing in the spice and textile trades."

Of course, Templeton had.

Aubriella's hazel gaze swept to Jack's face.

"I'm contemplating several ventures right now." He had made no commitments and, in truth, wasn't certain he wanted to take on additional undertakings. He passed Aubriella a glass of wine. "Your father asked me to deliver this to you."

Mr. Penford hadn't, but the little white lie protected her from the curious glances speared in her direction at his kindness. It took little to stir the gossipmongers into a frenzy of speculation, and White's betting book overflowed with nonsensical conjecture.

Having worked for every cent he had acquired, Jack had no use for gambling and even less respect for those who wasted funds on frivolous wagers. Men lost fortunes on everything from horse races to the tumbling of dice and bets as ludicrous as whether a rat would escape with a crust of bread or a lady would drop her handkerchief for a certain gentleman.

The women were little better and, in many cases, worse.

Lives ruined, estates impoverished, children neglected, individuals forced into arranged marriages and marriages of convenience, all because of a feckless need to win. On the rare occasion Jack indulged in a wager, it never involved money or property. At the end of the night, the most he'd owe was a bottle of brandy or a free meal at one of his restaurants.

His wastrel Uncle Martin, Earl of Marchant, had all but bankrupted the earldom, and his three sons practically prostituted themselves into loveless marriages to heiresses to fill the family's hollow coffers once more. Jack's mother had fallen in love with a gambling sot who had sent the family to the poorhouse for a time.

Both his parents had died in that hellhole, leaving him to care for his younger brother.

Jack never intended to be a pauper again, nor would he follow in his rakehell father's footsteps. Toward that end, he eschewed the same temptations, and even though he could've increased his and Duncan's fortunes exponentially by adding gaming rooms to his restaurants or turning them into gaming hells, he refused to do so.

Money dishonorably earned was tainted. Funds gained by hard work, shrewdness, or others' ineptness, on the other hand…

"Thank you." Aubriella angled her long neck to meet his gaze as she sipped. "Papa is *most* considerate."

She knew as well as Jack did that he fibbed.

Mrs. Templeton had set aside a separate salon for card and dice games—but only for forfeit prizes. Mrs. Templeton didn't allow gambling for profit in her grand home. Wise lady.

"This afternoon, after I posed for your sketching, you promised me a game of hazard, Miss Penford." That wasn't entirely true. She hadn't asked him to sit for her. Her talent was such that she could quickly sketch a scene, image, or person and had done so while the others labored over a single drawing.

Neither had she promised him a toss of the dice.

"Please excuse me." She rose and, graceful as a swan, skirted an armchair.

Jack extended his arm, and after the merest hesitation, she slid her gloved hand into the crook. After taking a casual sip of wine, she glanced at him from the corner of her eyes.

"I don't recall promising you to play hazard," she said.

He winked as they strolled toward the card room. "It was the only excuse I could think of at the spur of the moment to save you."

She rolled her eyes. "I didn't need saving."

"We all need saving at some time or other." He grinned down at her.

"Jack." A female titter accompanied the calling of his name. "That is, Mr. Matherfield."

SEVEN

Still in the corridor

Hell's clanging bells.

Jack stiffened and, with reluctance in every bone and muscle, turned toward Francine Willoughby, lingering near a corner alcove.

Had the wench been lying in wait for him?

Eager to sink her claws into the man she hoped would be her husband?

Not if purple unicorns danced in hell with bells on their painted hooves.

She raked a condescending glance over Aubriella, her cat-like eyes narrowing in poorly hidden jealousy.

"Have you spoken to my father?" Miss Willoughby asked without a hint of chagrin.

Miss Willoughby had gall. Jack would give her that. If she hoped to cause a public scene, she'd better think again.

"I shall allow you a moment." Face pale, Aubriella moved to withdraw her hand from Jack's arm, but he pulled it close to his ribs, preventing her escape.

She should never feel as if she must flee the likes of unremarkable and wholly forgettable Francine Willoughby.

"No need for you to leave." Jack pinned Francine Willoughby with a contemptuous glare, pointedly lowering his focus to her still-flat belly before meeting her uncertain eyes.

Laughter stretched into the passageway from the cardroom, and someone ran their fingers over the pianoforte's keys.

Speaking low, he said, "Your vile ploy did not work. Your father is taking you back to London. Tonight."

She gasped, flinging a hand to her throat.

"*London*? Tonight? No. That's not—" Eyes blazing with madness, she shook her head, the dark brown ringlets framing her face bouncing from her vehemence. "Papa said… He promised me that you—"

As if realizing she'd let slip a secret, she cleared her throat and looked around frantically.

"I don't care what *he* promised," Jack snapped, barely keeping his frayed emotional tether in check. "I shall not be coerced, blackmailed, or manipulated into doing anything I do not want to do and assuredly not for something I am *not* responsible for."

Francine's complexion went waxen, but desperate and perhaps slightly dicked in the knob, she persisted. "I'll make a scene. Cause a ruckus the likes of which the *haut ton* has never seen before."

Not likely. She wasn't the first and certainly wouldn't be the last chit to find herself with child outside wedlock.

"No, I don't think you will." Aubriella stepped forward. "Several days ago, someone created a bet that you would wed within a month. People have wagered upon the outcome."

Jack pinned her with a speculative glance.

They have?

Just how did she come to know about this bet?

Her tone kind but firm, Aubriella dropped her attention to Francine's middle before raising her eyes to meet the other woman's. "I am certain you do not want the *reason* for that wager to become public. For your sake, go back to London with your father. Better yet, retire to the country or go abroad for several months or a year."

Francine's mouth worked, but no sound emerged. Posture defiant and murder spewing from her eyes, she spun on her satin heels and stomped down the corridor.

"Somehow, I doubt we've seen the last of her," Aubriella murmured, her eyebrows pulled into a vee across her nose. "She's quite desperate and unwilling to give up easily. Or else she wouldn't be here. I'd guess prospective husbands have been hard to find. She might well have to leave the country for a year and pretend to be widowed when she returns."

There was much truth to her honest, but not spiteful, observation.

"Tell me, Aubriella. Where did you come by the information regarding the wager about Miss Willoughby's delicate condition?" Jack steered her into the alcove Francine had vacated and flicked one side of the drapery down, ensconcing them in muted half-light. "And I'll have the truth, if you please."

Canting her head, Aubriella narrowed her eyes, astute intelligence gleaming in their depths. "I'll tell you after our game of hazard. If you win, that is."

Sly minx.

"And if you win?" She wouldn't because Jack was a master at probability and numbers and knew precisely when to quit.

She eyed him up and down with provocative intensity, and being the virile man he was, his body responded predictably. And that proved most unexpected and disturbing.

"Should I prevail, Jack, you'll allow me to draw you, wearing only your pantaloons."

EIGHT

Still in the alcove

Several shocked seconds later

"*What*?" Jack blinked owlishly.

Aubriella had utterly flummoxed him.

"What?" he repeated, pulling on his earlobe. "Surely I misheard you."

"You heard me perfectly well, Jackson Matherfield. You will allow me to draw you, front, back, and sides, in various poses and donned only in pantaloons." Aubriella was quite certain that of all the things she might have chosen as a stake, Jack had never considered such an outrageous and scandalous request.

But how else could she acquire a fit male specimen to compare to da Vinci's renderings?

Desperate times and all that.

His expression a mixture of horrified mirth and offense, Jack stared so long, Aubriella began to reconsider her impulsiveness. At last, he spoke, the usual sardonic man she'd come to expect.

"May I surmise, Aubrie, that your obsession with the human body has not waned over time?"

"It has not, though I wouldn't call it an obsession but a keen scientific interest." On the verge of blurting that she possessed da Vinci's drawings of human anatomy, she bit her lip.

Could she trust Jack with her disreputable secret?

No.

Not yet, at least.

After all, he'd exposed Aubriella's stunt at university and, just like every other male she knew, had deemed it unfitting for a woman to pursue knowledge of biology and anatomy. As if women weren't capable of knowing their own minds and interests.

"No. I cannot agree, and I shan't apologize for refusing." He shook his head, a shock of ebony hair falling over his forehead. "Emmet would call me out. You'd be ruined. Besides, where in the bloody hell do you think you could sketch me without discovery?"

Jack had a valid point there, but Aubriella refused to concede.

"I suspected you'd refuse." She lifted a shoulder, pretending a nonchalance she didn't feel. "I guess you'll never know how I came by the knowledge regarding The Honorable Francine Willoughby."

She had no intention of revealing the truth to him. The *Ladies of Opportunity* had sworn a solemn oath to preserve their clients' privacy.

Still, Jack didn't know that.

"Besides, I'm positive you'd lose." She permitted a confident upsweep of her lips. "I haven't been bested at hazard in years. I'm sure it would bruise your male pride to lose to a mere woman—a gangly, clumsy, bluestocking spinster to boot."

"Don't do that," Jack snapped, censure darkening his features.

Aubriella couldn't prevent her eyes from flying wide at his unexpected terseness. "Do what?"

"Disparage yourself." He raked a hand through his hair, then gently clasped her shoulders. "You are a lovely young woman with a figure any man with eyes in his head would admire. What's more, you are intelligent—the most intelligent woman I am acquainted with. You do not need artifice or pretentiousness, and I have never heard you speak unkindly of anyone nor spread gossip."

He'd painted her a virtual saint.

Nevertheless, Aubriella barely heard the compliments. At his touch, sensation zipped along her arms, and though it made no sense scientifically, her knees went weak, and lightheadedness swept through her.

Surely hunger explained this curious physical response.

She'd scarcely touched luncheon or dinner.

"I…" She swallowed; her mouth suddenly gone dry as cold ashes. Rarely at a loss for words, she struggled to gather her scattered wits. "I only repeated what others have said."

"Well, don't." Jack squeezed her shoulders and then let loose. "Whoever said such stupid things is an idiot and unworthy of your regard. Don't listen to them."

"*You've* said those things, Jack."

And more hurtful remarks she would prefer not to dredge up.

She'd heard him once when he'd been speaking to Emmet.

And yes, Aubriella had overheard others as well over

the years. At first, the insults and derisions stung something awful, but in time, she'd grown a thicker skin, and other than an occasional prick now and then, she'd become almost immune to them.

A stricken expression shadowed the lean contours and planes of his striking features. He searched Aubriella's face, shame and regret softening the corners of his eyes. "Then *I'm* an idiot. I have no excuse to offer but can only beg your forgiveness."

"It was a long time ago. Think no more on it." Why she should pardon him now, when for years she'd held his words against him, made no sense whatsoever. But much about Jackson Matherfield made no sense of late.

He extended his forefinger and, after a moment's hesitation, grazed the rough pad over her left cheek, then across her upper lip. "You are incomparable. A lily amongst ferns."

"*Lily?*" A giggle escaped Aubriella, and she flicked a bit of lint off his jacket. "Jack, you're waxing poetic. I never thought I'd see the day when the sardonic, cynical Jackson Matherfield concocted nonsensical platitudes."

A severe scowl lashed his eyebrows together.

"Do not change the subject, Aubrie. You've believed yourself undesirable for too long, and you keep others at a distance to protect yourself."

Aubriella folded her arms and tapped the toes of her right foot. She didn't know what to do with this new, sensitive, kind Jack. The old Jack, the teasing, taunting rogue she could handle.

But this one?

Jackson Matherfield confused the very devil out of her, and Aubriella didn't like being perplexed.

"In case you hadn't noticed, gentlemen haven't exactly been lining up to court me." No one ever had eyes for her when her sisters outshone her like the sun to a candle.

"I'm four and twenty, Jack. Firmly on the shelf. I appreciate your kindness. I do, but you needn't flatter me or manufacture compliments. You know full well that I'm not like other females. I don't require a man's approval, nor am I distraught because I'm not desirable and shall never marry."

Perhaps the tiniest bit troubled that she wasn't pretty or sought after, but she'd walk on hot coals before admitting that to him.

"Bugger that bloody balderdash." Before she could scold him for his coarse language—which she didn't really mind—or comment on his unintended alliteration, Jack snaked an iron-like arm around her waist and the other across her shoulders, pulling her tight against him in an unbreakable embrace.

Her pulse accelerated with excitement and anticipation.

"I'll show you just how desirable you are, Aubrie."

A second later, his firm mouth covered hers in a smoldering kiss, so scorching and potent she had to clutch his shoulders to remain standing.

Lord, have mercy.

Electricity sluiced through her as a headiness she'd never imagined engulfed her from the soles of her feet to the crown of her head.

When his tongue nudged her mouth open and tangled with hers, Aubriella was lost. She gave up trying to make sense of what was happening and let logic, reason, and common sense flit away until all that remained was Jack and a haze of passion, need, and want.

He pressed his powerful body into hers, his muscles flexing beneath her hands. His intoxicating cologne engulfed her.

And his mouth.

Oh, his magnificent mouth and the magic he wrought with his lips.

Raucous masculine laughter nearby made him lift his head.

Aubriella slowly forced her weighted eyelids open, her gaze meshing with his.

Eyes hooded and heavy with passion, he cupped her face. "Never say you are undesirable again. Never."

At that moment, Aubriella felt like the most beautiful, alluring woman on earth, and hot tears pricked her eyelids. She hadn't realized how bereft she was, and now that she'd experienced desire, she didn't know if she could go on as if nothing had changed.

Everything had changed.

In truth, she very much feared Jackson Matherfield had altered her life forever.

Overcome with bashfulness, she curved her mouth into a small, fragile smile. "Will you let me draw you? I shan't include your face, so no one will know who it is."

Closing his eyes, he threw his head back, exposing the strong column of his throat, and groaned.

"You will be the death of me, Aubriella Penford."

Sighing, he set her away from him and straightened her earring.

"We'll leave it to the dice, vixen. If you win, I'll let you sketch me, though God only knows how we'll manage it. If I win, you'll tell me what you know about the mysterious wager regarding Miss Willoughby and how you came to know it. Agreed?"

This might very well be her only chance to see the male form and sketch it. And suddenly, it had become very important that it was Jack that she drew. Aubriella refused to examine the reason behind that newfound need. "Agreed, but no one else can know the stakes. As far as they are concerned, we're playing for a forfeit."

"That is wise. Shall we? We have dice to cast unless you'd settle for a game of vingt-et-un instead?" He cocked an eyebrow.

In expectation?

In challenge?

Her mind kept wandering to that blistering kiss.

How was she supposed to concentrate now?

Was that the rogue's intent all along?

Had he planned to kiss her, to disarm her?

Would Jack do something that underhanded?

Aubriella's gut said no, but what did she really know about men and their ways?

She considered his suggestion. Vingt-et-un was far simpler to play than hazard. She mentally weighed the chances of winning at either game and settled on hazard, although, in all honesty, games of chance were wholly unreliable. "I think we'll stick with the dice."

"The game will be a first for us," he said. "Even though we've attended many of the same events, including the Templetons' annual house party, many times."

His point?

Jack extended his elbow. "Tonight seems to be fraught with new experiences."

Would Aubriella remember this yuletide toss of the dice as the exact moment her life irrevocably changed? Or had it happened when Jack had kissed her, and for the first time in a very long while, she admitted she wanted more out of life than studying scientific specimens and drawings?

She wanted passion and love.

And she feared that newfound discovery mightn't ever be fulfilled.

NINE

Templetons' card room

TWENTY MINUTES LATER

AFTER WAITING fifteen minutes for two places to open up at an existing hazard table and realizing that no one seemed inclined to leave, Jack requested a pair of dice from a footman. The fellow cheerfully complied, and Jack pocketed the pieces. Since the wager was between him and Aubriella, they needn't play in the card room.

Any small table—preferably in a quiet nook in a public room—would suffice.

More unsettled by their kiss than he cared to admit, Jack couldn't risk being alone with her again. He'd never intended to kiss her, but something had unfurled inside him once he had. Something dormant had awakened and bludgeoned him with untenable desire.

Emmet might kill him for overstepping, and rightly so.

Aubriella had Jack at sixes and sevens. That was

ironic since the expression came from hazard, the very game they intended to engage in shortly.

Kissing Aubriella was a mistake that mustn't happen again.

Nevertheless, he wouldn't embarrass them both by telling her so.

Unfortunately and unpreventably, he suspected she'd assume his reluctance to kiss her again stemmed from him not finding her desirable when the opposite was true. He was at a loss to explain the powerful, potent reaction after all these years they'd known each other.

Jack had kissed women before—one didn't get to be thirty and never kissed a woman. Many ladies of all stations had wanted to join with him. However, even as a randy youth, he'd held an old-fashioned belief that coupling should involve more than mere physical satisfaction. That notion wasn't popular among any social class, so he kept the belief to himself.

He, a successful business owner and considered a man about town, would be a laughingstock should his secret become known.

That Aubriella should be the woman who tempted him to put aside the stricture guiding his sexual conduct these many years was a monumental conundrum. He'd only intended to prove that she was a desirable woman. Now, he'd become entangled in the web of his own making, and he had no idea how to escape except to avoid her, which he could not do.

Not after he'd vowed to stay by her side.

The next fortnight might prove to be the most troublesome and perplexing of his life, and he suspected his self-control was about to be tested mightily. He grasped her elbow, and she glanced up at him. A freckle to the right of her mouth taunted Jack, begging him to kiss the speck, and the one below her right ear beseeched him to nuzzle her slender neck.

Lord, he was in trouble.

Monumental, colossal, overwhelming trouble.

Mayhap he should reconsider his celibate state.

Except the plain, bitter truth was, no woman but Aubriella would do. At some point, he'd have to examine that peculiarity, but not now. At this moment, he had a wager to win and to discover how she knew of Francine Willoughby's delicate condition when scandalous secrets like that were well guarded.

"Jack?" A cute frown puckered Aubriella's forehead and wrinkled her nose. "Are you well? You look as if you are not feeling quite the thing."

"Yes, quite well." Clearing his throat, Jack cast a hasty glance around the noisy room. Several of his friends, including Shelby Tellinger and Robyn Fitzlloyd, were engaged in games of whist, piquet, or loo. He vowed that tonight's guests had swelled to well over forty—likely closer to fifty.

Given the Templetons often invited their neighbors for the evening events during the house party, that was a distinct possibility. Duncan had yet to reappear unless he was in the drawing room from whence a male-female duet, accompanied by a pianoforte, filtered forth.

Of the Willoughbys, there was no sign, and hopefully, that portended their unexpected and rapid departure from Stockworth Manor.

"Offhand, do you know where we might play our game that affords us privacy but is within the bounds of propriety?" Jack steered Aubriella toward the paneled door to the corridor.

She nodded. "The library if we leave the door open? If I recall, there's a table in the center we could pull chairs near."

Aubriella smiled as her younger sister in virginal white—flushed with pleasure and seated at a nearby table surrounded by swains—fluttered her fingers toward her before flipping over her card and letting out a delighted squeal.

Dutiful mother and chaperone, Mrs. Penford, sat chatting along the wall with two other matrons. No doubt exchanging motherly boasts about their offspring. She gave her youngest an indulgent smile before angling her head to listen to the lady on her left.

Had Mrs. Penford even noticed Aubriella's entrance and now pending exit?

Something very much like exasperation kicked Jack's ribs at her oblivious neglect of her middle daughter. Granted, at four and twenty, Aubriella didn't require constant supervision as Jessamine did, but having observed the family for several years, the Penford's indifference toward their second daughter bordered on neglect.

No wonder Aubriella had found hobbies to occupy herself. Inappropriate hobbies, to be sure. But then, what did her negligent parents care?

Aubriella might have hidden shocking drawings of nudes in her wardrobe, and the Penfords would've remained blissfully unaware. As long as she didn't cause them any inconvenience or embarrassment, she was all but invisible.

A chorus of congratulations erupted at Miss Jessamine's table.

At once, three chaps rose and began strutting around the room, flapping their arms, bobbing their heads, and crowing. Easy to discern what that forfeit had been. Jack knew from experience that the forfeitures would become increasingly daring and naughty as the house party progressed.

"The library it is." The hubbub faded as he and Aubriella strolled toward the back of the house. On his arm, Aubriella relaxed and breathed a little easier with each passing step.

These assemblies truly taxed her.

He'd noticed her distress before but never thought to ask why. He'd always assumed social ineptness kept her to herself. Most of the time, she was nowhere to be found. She disappeared for most of the event and reappeared as it drew to an end.

"Why do you dislike gatherings so much, Aubriella?"

Jack slowed his pace as he glanced down at her. The crown of her head just reached his shoulder, and tonight, someone had woven white silk ribbons through her shiny, coiffed tresses.

The flickering candles in the brass wall sconces cast shadows across her face when she turned to look up at him.

His breath stalled for a heartbeat.

Why couldn't others see her beauty?

Wide eyes in an oval face, full pink lips, and a slightly upturned nose. The freckles smattering Aubriella's porcelain skin merely added to her allure—particularly that beauty mark near her mouth which would drive him crazy with want from now until forever.

"I don't dislike them, per se. I simply do not fit in. I feel rather like a goat asked to participate in the Ascot horse race. Of course, I can run the track, but my gait is awkward. I'm not a sleek beauty, and I have no chance of winning. My gaucheness causes unintentional amusement, and no one appreciates being laughed at."

"I told you not to belittle yourself." Jack turned her toward him and raised her chin with his forefinger instead of pulling her into his protective embrace and kissing her forehead as he yearned to do.

No more kisses, he reminded himself sternly.

Aubriella had disdained herself for so long that she couldn't see her own appeal.

"I shall have to demand a forfeit each time you do." He winked to soften the words.

A kiss would do nicely.

No. No more kisses.

Twice in as many seconds, Jack had to remind himself of his vow, and that spelled eventual failure.

Perhaps unexpected urgent business required his attention in London.

Which was worse?

Breaking his word or kissing her?

She pulled a face and poked him in the chest. Hard. "You asked, you dolt. I explained the best way I knew how. And if you ever tease me about it, I'll… well, I'll draw you with three nipples."

TEN

Halfway to the Templetons' library

JACK THREW BACK his head and laughed—deep, unfettered amusement at her silly, but likely genuine, threat.

What other female would say such a thing?

"You'll have to win first, Aubrie."

"I assure you, Jackson Matherfield. I shall." Finding her rare confidence amusing and estimable, he almost hoped she would prevail.

Almost.

They finished the short trek to the library in silence.

In short order, Jack pulled two comfortably worn burgundy velvet library chairs trimmed in gold braid beside an octagonal marble-topped inlaid table. After lighting the tapers in a gilt brass three-branch candelabra from the low-burning hearth fire, Aubriella set it in the table's middle.

Giving a satisfied nod and checking to ensure the door stood open, she slipped into one chair without waiting for him to pull it out. "Shall we begin?"

The ugly-as-sin chinoiserie mantel clock with a blue foo dog top, chimed quarter past eleven.

How had it become so late?

"Indeed. The hour grows advanced." He pulled the ivory dice from his pocket and offered them to her. "Best two out of three?"

It seemed unfair only to give her a single chance when he was certain of the outcome.

"If you think *you* need that many," she quipped with a mischievous smile.

Comfortable silence descended, punctuated by the clock *tick-tocking* on the carved mahogany mantel, the fire lazily crackling and hissing, and the dice clattering against the marble inlays.

Jack won the first game, but not without breaking a sweat. It had been a far closer match than he'd anticipated, as had the second in which Aubriella triumphed.

He'd underestimated her.

Her forehead furrowed in concentration as she rolled the dice between her hands.

"I choose seven as my main," she said.

If she rolled a seven—a nicks—on her first toss this third game, it was over.

She won.

Jack would shed his clothing for her—God help them both. Not that the idea didn't have merit, but the consequences didn't bear contemplating. Unless he cried off, which was the sensible thing to do.

His honor prohibited him from keeping his word, and his deuced honor also forbade him to pose for her nearly unclothed. She'd backed him into a corner. No, his stupidity and cockiness had caused this conundrum.

Grinning, he shook his head. "Neither of us has a throw in on the first roll. The probability is quite low."

"Yes, but a seven has a slightly greater chance." Voices in the corridor made her glance toward the door. "How shall we explain playing in here, rather than the card room, should someone come upon us?"

"We can say you wanted to practice before joining a game in the card room." She didn't need practice, but Jack doubted anyone would question the fabrication.

"I suppose that suffices." Filling her lungs with air, which caused her bosom to swell quite nicely, she closed her eyes and moved her mouth in silent prayer before kissing her fist.

"Please."

"You seem quite desperate to see me unclothed." Jack leaned back in his chair; one arm slung over the back. "I believe I should be scandalized."

"Oh, pish posh." She wrinkled her nose, causing the smattering of freckles to dance. "It takes much more than disrobing to shock you. Besides, any fit man would suffice."

The voices grew louder.

A man and woman argued passionately, though they were still too far away for Aubriella to discern their words.

Jack jutted his chin toward the entrance. "I fear we are about to be interrupted."

Lips pressed tight, Aubriella opened her hand, and the dice tumbled off her fingertips.

The first rolled to a stop.

A six.

She stood little chance of winning, but he still held his breath.

The second tumbled a little farther.

And a one.

Bloody hell.

She'd done it, by Jove.

He ought to be vexed.

Instead, Jack was pleased for her, even if he found himself in a deuced pickle.

"I won," Aubriella breathed, half in awe and half in delight. She lifted her bright eyes to Jack's. "*I won.* You have to let me sketch you. And I want to do it while we're here. It will be easier to go unnoticed."

Bollocks.

He thought he'd have until they returned to London to devise a location or renege. He grunted. "I'll have the why of that strange wager about Miss Willoughby one way or the other."

"It's nothing. I assure you." She made a flapping motion with her hand as she collected the dice.

Her too-innocent demeanor didn't fool him. Aubriella was an atrocious actress and a worse liar.

"It's not *nothing* when the chit tried to force me to marry her," he retorted with more heat than intended.

Aubriella's expression grew shuttered, and if she'd slammed the doors and locked them, she couldn't have been clearer. Their amiable interlude had ended, and she'd retreated to cool aloofness again.

"I saw you together last year, and from what I observed, you weren't exactly impartial to her overtures." Accusation and censure threaded her tone, now as frigid as the Arctic.

Jack racked his brain.

When could Aubriella have seen him?

That certainly explained her don't-come-near-me-leper-attitude these past months.

Her color high, she slid a glance to the door. "I only interjected earlier because I dislike anyone being bullied or manipulated. Still, if you *are* responsible..."

"I am *not* responsible for Francine's condition. In fact, I've avoided her like the plague after she practically accosted me in the conservatory during last year's Christmastide house party." He curled his lip in disgust. "Is that where you saw us?"

Jack couldn't very well tell Aubriella he was a virgin. Not only did he doubt she'd believe him, it was wholly inappropriate.

Expression taut, Aubriella gave a tense dip of her chin. "I left at once, of course."

"If you'd stayed, you would've seen me scold her for her forwardness and make it clear I had no interest in her and never would before—"

Footsteps—rapid, angry tread fall—echoed outside the library door, and Jack had just swiveled to look over his shoulder when Roxina Danforth and Shelby Tellinger plowed in, one after the other.

"Elli?" Miss Danforth came up short, and Tellinger bumped into her, almost sending her to the floor. He grabbed her arm to steady her, but she jerked away as if he'd scalded her.

Her glare would've incinerated another man on the spot, but Tellinger merely returned her scowl and stepped around her.

Those two were constantly at odds.

What set them off this evening?

"Are we interrupting?" Tellinger could see blasted well that they were.

Nevertheless, Jack rose and pocketed the dice. "No, we've just finished. Miss Penford wanted a private hazard lesson before she undertook a game with others."

"But, Elli is—" Miss Danforth clamped her mouth shut, giving her friend an I-don't-know-what-is-going-but-I'm-keeping-my-mouth-closed look.

Jack applauded her loyalty.

Tellinger planted a hand on his hip, his impatience

for Jack and Aubriella to leave palpable. "Ah, well then. I wish you luck, Miss Penford."

"I can stay." Aubriella touched Miss Danforth's forearm. "If you wish."

To her credit, though white lines bracketed her mouth, Miss Danforth didn't drag her friend into the fray. "Not a bit of it, dearest. Go along. I simply need to disabuse Mr. Tellinger of a misconception."

Tellinger snorted, barely suppressed ire radiating from him.

"I can stay as well." Jack wasn't about to leave a woman alone with a man as angry as Tellinger.

"Oh, for the love of God." Tellinger stomped across the room to stand before the waning fire and stare into the coals. "I simply want to know where her profligate brother has skulked off to."

As up to this moment, Tellinger had been Mitchel Danforth's closest friend, his hostility toward Danforth came as quite a surprise.

"It's quite all right, Mr. Matherfield. Aubriella." The epitome of sereneness, Miss Danforth folded her hands across her abdomen, though she couldn't quite control her timorous smile. "I only need a few moments with Mr. Tellinger. I promise you. I shall join you before I'm missed."

"I'm not going to harm her," Tellinger muttered as he faced them. "She'll be along in five minutes. If not, feel free to return and call me to task."

Aubriella nibbled her lower lip in indecision. "Are you quite sure, Zina?"

Pursing her lips and casting Tellinger an annoyed glance, Miss Danforth nodded.

As Jack followed Aubriella from the library, Tellinger demanded, "Where is he, Roxina? Where is Mitchel?"

ELEVEN

Still in Templetons' library

*Several tense tick-tocks **of the mantel clock later***

FOLDING her arms tightly to her chest, Roxina pressed her lips together against the unladylike oath she longed to hurl at Shelby Tellinger. If she were a man, she'd punch his arrogant face and rearrange that perfectly straight nose for calling her a liar.

How dare he humiliate her in front of her dearest friend and Jackson Matherfield?

How odd to come upon Aubriella and Matherfield in the library.

Roxina knew full well that Aubriella had no liking for Jack. And that twaddle about teaching her hazard? Aubriella was a dab hand at the game. She didn't need any instruction or practice.

No, something was too smoky by far.

Regardless, Roxina would deal with that business later.

She eyed Shelby from beneath her lashes.

Right now, she must face Shelby Tellinger, more infuriated than she'd ever witnessed him before. He'd been his usual standoffish, brooding self this morning. This evening, however, something had sent him into a proper froth.

Taking three deep breaths and counting to five with each inhalation and exhalation, as she taught herself when Mitchel was in one of his rages, she brought her racing heart and pulse under control. Raised voices, particularly males, nearly always caused her extreme anxiety. It brought back terrifying memories of her father shouting at Mama.

Mustering her equanimity and forcing calmness to her voice, she met Shelby's infuriated glacial gray eyes.

"I told you, Shelby. I don't know where Mitchel is. You, above all people, are aware he does not include me in his confidence. My brother lives his life, and I live mine. Actually, I'm surprised you don't know where he's off to. I thought you were chums and shared *everything*."

Her sarcasm earned her another eviscerating scowl.

"Mitchel was remarkably closemouthed about his holiday plans. I presume he intended…" Shelby rubbed a long finger beneath his nose because no doubt what he'd intended to say was not meant for delicate ears. "Well, that he wanted seclusion and privacy."

She rested a hip on the sofa's arm. "Mitchel meant to engage in a season of holiday cheer and whoring?"

He didn't appear shocked at her crude question, so then why pretend it wasn't true?

Mitchel was the worst sort of profligate scoundrel.

Angling her head, she narrowed her eyes. "Or, perhaps, cuckolding some poor fellow."

"I am not his keeper." Tellinger laced his fingers

behind his back, but his granite jaw belied his false tranquility. "Neither am I his confessor or conscience."

Roxina had never seen him in such a state. Like a caged lion or panther, ready to spring upon its prey. Perched as she was on the sofa's arm—mostly because her too-small second-hand shoes pinched her toes, and her feet were killing her—he seemed taller than his six feet, two inches as he towered above her.

"Well, I certainly am none of those either," she retorted with equal rancor.

Suddenly weary, she placed a palm against her forehead where a niggling ache portended a migraine if she didn't promptly find her bed. "I think he left around the thirteenth, but I cannot be sure. He rarely sleeps at the Gloucester Street house, and I only see him in passing every couple of weeks or so. I noticed his bedchamber door ajar, and clothing was strewn about as if he'd packed in haste."

"Blast him to Hades." Shelby paced away five steps, then stamped back to glower down at her. "I *must* find him."

Roxina sighed and permitted her shoulders to slump an inch. "Why? What has he done that has caused you, his dearest friend, to turn on him?"

Did she really want to know?

"I am *not* his dearest friend. I watch him closely because he is an untrustworthy blackguard, and that is better done by spending time with him."

"*Oh.*" The breath left Roxina's lungs in a rush.

What did she say to that confession?

"He impersonated me and forged my signature." Shelby released a frustrated huff and scraped a hand through his dark blond hair. "He used my name and character to obtain a thousand-pound loan from a card sharp, which came due the fifteenth. The henchmen came round to collect yesterday. My butler promptly penned me a message."

"Good Lord." Roxina's blood ran cold before she flushed with heat. "Mitchel is selfish and untrustworthy but to betray you in such a fashion…"

She spread her hands.

"I am truly sorry, Shelby."

A thousand pounds.

A veritable fortune.

Could Shelby afford to pay the loan?

The consequences, if he couldn't, might be dire.

He quirked a hawkish dark blond eyebrow. "I don't suppose he has any funds or valuables at the house?"

She laughed; the sound almost hysterical to her ears.

"If he had, don't you think I would've used them to pay the baker? Butcher? Grocer?" She gestured toward her gown. "Perhaps splurged and bought a couple of yards of fabric to make a new gown? This travesty was my mother's, Shelby, and she's been dead for a decade. I've remade this rag four times, and no one here isn't aware of my reduced circumstances."

If it weren't for the earnings from the *Ladies of Opportunity*'s betting book, she'd have starved long ago.

On the verge of tears, she swallowed and blinked rapidly.

I shall not cry in front of him.

Not *him.*

Shelby Tellinger, who had befriended the monster who tormented Roxina her entire life. Since the moment she came into the world and stripped her fourteen-year-old half-brother of his only child status, he'd put every effort into making her life miserable to pay for robbing him of that prestigious position.

Shelby sank onto the sofa and crossed one long leg over the other. Drumming his fingertips on the brocade arm, he contemplated her with such intensity that Roxina fidgeted and then stood.

"Well, if that is all, I shall excuse myself." And make straight for her bed. Although, how she would sleep with the news Shelby just imparted, she couldn't fathom.

"That is not all, Roxina."

Of course, it wasn't.

"He's mortgaged your house to the hilt. I purchased the loan six years ago so you wouldn't be evicted."

Oh, my God.

It cannot be true.

But Roxina knew, deep in her soul, Shelby spoke the truth.

Her head spun, and she extended a hand to grasp hold of something so she wouldn't crumple to the floor in a hysterical heap. She had a smattering of pride left, and to let Shelby Tellinger see her come undone—she couldn't bear it.

Shelby shot to his feet and wrapped an arm around her shoulder. Far gentler than she believed him capable of being, he guided her to the sofa.

"Sit down, Roxina. You've had a terrible shock."

She licked her lower lip, afraid she might cast up her accounts. "You bought the mortgage?"

Six years ago?

Wasn't that about the time he and Mitchel had become friends?

So, he had spoke the truth about their quasi friendship, too.

He gave a terse nod. "I knew he was a spendthrift and wouldn't make the payments. And I also knew he didn't give a tinker's damn if he left you without a home."

Tears burned behind her eyelids.

She'd been so awful to Shelby, and he proved himself a more decent human than her own flesh and blood.

He sat beside her and took her hand in his.

"I shall have to use the house and contents as collateral, Roxina. Not only haven't I the cash to repay the loan at present, but I don't have time to sell the house either. The type of people Mitchel borrowed from won't wait until I can raise the funds. Until I can locate your brother and bring charges against him, I have no choice. Even then, it's not likely I'll recover any of the money."

"Use the house as collateral?" She could barely force the words past her stiff lips. "What will become of me? Where will I go? I have no living relatives."

"I shall think of something." For the first time that evening, he directed a genuine smile toward her. "Trust me, Roxina."

Trust *him*?

A man she'd loathed for years?

He passed her a crisp, neatly folded, and starched handkerchief. "Here."

So lost in misery and fear, Roxina hadn't been aware tears trailed down her cheeks. She accepted the cloth—it smelled of sandalwood and cloves and him—and patted her face.

"I suggest you use discretion who you share this information with." Kindness glinted in his eyes, warming them to a dove-gray shade. "We wouldn't want to put a pall on the festivities."

"Of course." Roxina doubted she'd be able to enjoy the next two weeks. Especially knowing she'd shortly have nowhere to live. But she wouldn't ruin the occasion for the others.

She stood on wobbly legs, Shelby's handkerchief wadded in her fist.

"I'll return your handkerchief after it's laundered." She'd wash it herself as she couldn't afford the vails the other guests paid the servants. Her friends passed the expected coins to the domestics on her behalf.

She wore humiliation and chagrin like a second skin these days.

"It's of no import." He also stood, concern pleating the corners of his eyes.

She drew in a ragged breath.

"Thank you. I…" A fresh wave of tears threatened to engulf her, but Roxina swallowed them down. Shelby Tellinger would not see her weep again. "Please excuse me. I have a headache and need to lie down."

"I am sorry, Roxina. Truly I am."

Grief clogged her throat, and she could only nod as she fled the library and tore to the bedchamber, praying she didn't encounter anyone along the way.

All this time, she'd loathed the man who had ensured she had a place to live.

TWELVE

Stockworth Manor conservatory

THE NEXT DAY — AFTERNOON

AUBRIELLA ROVED her gaze around the large conservatory, seeking an ideal location to sketch Jack. Perhaps over there, against the backdrop of potted Ficus and ferns. With enough candles strategically arranged, the lighting should be sufficient.

She'd decided the greenhouse was the most logical place to carry out her daring plan. To draw the various poses she desired, Aubriella estimated she'd need four to six hours, which meant at least two nights, mayhap three, of clandestine sneaking back and forth.

Jack wouldn't be happy, and she fully expected he'd refuse more than a single night. She'd cross that hurdle when it arose. Nevertheless, not only was the solar warm —she didn't want him goose fleshed and shivering—but late at night, it wasn't likely anyone would interrupt them, including Francine.

She and her father had departed Stockworth Manor last evening without bidding their hosts farewell. No great loss there. What was a loss was Roxina's presence. She'd pleaded a headache when Aubriella had retired last night and refused to leave their shared chamber today.

In truth, her friend appeared quite ill, though she refused Aubriella's offer to send for a physician. When Aubriella had peeked in on Roxina an hour ago, she'd been asleep in the darkened chamber. As soon as tea was over, Aubriella intended to check on her again. It wasn't like Roxina to remain abed.

Twice today, Shelby Tellinger approached Aubriella and inquired after Roxina.

That was most peculiar, since he usually distanced himself from Roxina. His concern was highly suspicious, and the more Aubriella considered it, the more she became convinced that not only was Roxina hiding in the bedchamber, she was hiding *something*. Something that caused her such distress that the typically stalwart Roxina refused to leave her chamber.

Aubriella meant to have the truth from her dearest friend.

With Jessamine's hand tucked in the crook of her elbow, the sisters and several others strolled the stone pavers, heated from beneath by a system of pipes linked to a wood furnace.

With its orange and lemon trees, pineapple plants, as well as several palms and other sun-loving vegetation, the greenhouse emitted a tropical atmosphere, which is exactly what Mabel had intended for this afternoon's tea. The idyllic scene starkly contrasted with the outdoors, where fluffy, wet snowflakes had started falling half an hour ago.

"Do you think the snow will stick, Elli?" Peering through the slightly foggy windows, Jessamine pulled her mazarine blue velvet pelisse's collar higher before glancing down at her impractical flared-heel, striped shoes.

"I honestly don't know, Minnie."

Aubriella hoped not.

Wasn't it a mere fortnight ago she prayed for snow and now asked the Good Lord for the opposite?

She didn't relish trudging from the manor house to the conservatory at midnight in a foot of snow. All in the name of science, of course. It didn't hurt that Jack was dreadfully handsome and possessed a Greek god's splendid physique. What else explained the taut fabric across his broad shoulders and long legs?

Jessamine formed a moue with her mouth.

On other girls, the pout seemed petulant, but the small turning down of Jessamine's lips gave her a fragile appearance rather than spoiled. "I shall ruin my new shoes for certain, and so shall you should we have to walk back to the house in the snow."

"Never fear, Miss Jessamine." Will Durham, one of Jessamine's most ardent admirers, sidled closer, not about to let such an opportunity pass. Reed thin and an inch shorter than Aubriella, he puffed out his chest.

An underweight robin or a bantam rooster.

"I shall be honored to carry you," he proudly pronounced.

Aubriella bit her tongue to keep from laughing at the comical image that presented. She would wager Mr. Durham couldn't lift a hay bale, let alone her sister, and Jessamine would find herself headfirst in a snowdrift.

"I'm sure that won't be necessary, Mr. Durham," Mama interjected before Aubriella or Jessamine could formulate a suitable response. Leave it to Mama to hone in on an over-eager suitor and firmly dissuade his zealous efforts to court Jessamine.

Aubriella slid a glance at the glass panels.

She doubted anyone would make it to the house without sodden footwear and damp hems.

A naughty, rebellious impulse made her shove her pointed-toe shoe outward a couple of inches and wiggle her foot. To test the waters, so to speak.

Would Will Durham notice?

She even cleared her throat. Quite noisily, in fact. A frog with croup would've sounded more ladylike.

Alas, her efforts proved futile.

Eyes only for Jessamine, Mr. Durham didn't extend the same invitation to her. Not that Aubriella would ever allow a man to tote her about like a bag of grain. Besides, no one ever died from cold, wet feet. Well, mayhap they had, but surely, she wouldn't catch the ague on the quarter-mile hike to the manor house.

If the need arose.

Even now, Mabel engaged in furtive conversation with several footmen near the conservatory entrance. She was probably arranging to ferry the guests back to the house.

Just once, Aubriella would like to have been the object of male attention, not her prettier sisters. It was stupid, silly, and irrational, but it did rather rub one's pride raw to be overlooked and ignored constantly.

Mama took Jessamine's elbow and half-turned away. "Come, dearest. I would like you to sit with me."

Ever the protective mama bear.

"What about Elli, Mama?" Compassion—or was it pity?—softened Jessamine's eyes.

Aubriella didn't like that one jot.

No, indeed.

Accustomed to being disregarded, she'd have found a seat in a quiet corner. However, having her younger self-absorbed sister notice their mother's negligence brought home just how insignificant Aubriella was.

"Elli?" Mama couldn't quite hide her befuddlement.

Yes, Mama. Your middle daughter. The one you generally deem inconsequential.

Mama swung back to face Aubriella. Seemingly as an afterthought, asked, "Do you wish to sit with us as well?"

She glanced behind her to the nearly full table where Papa, Lenora, and her husband already jabbered on about something or other with several guests.

Only Emmet was missing. Something had spooked his horse this morning when he dismounted, and he'd strained his ankle. Nothing serious, but he thought it wise to allow the swollen appendage to rest.

"I'm not sure there's room." Mama blinked, appearing rather flummoxed at what could hardly be considered a conundrum. Dear Mama. Never the brightest candle in the chandelier. "But you are so thin. I suppose we could squeeze in another chair."

"And *inconvenience* you?" Aubriella shook her head when her sarcasm didn't register. "I wouldn't think of it."

Just as they never thought of her.

She always managed on her own. Pain twinged behind her ribs, but she tamped down the emotion. She wouldn't wallow in self-pity. So, life hadn't handed her a basket of roses. That didn't mean she couldn't be happy.

Out of nowhere, Jack appeared at her side, smelling utterly marvelous, and for the umpteenth time in the past few days, she nearly sighed in relief. It wasn't wise to depend on him so much, but he had volunteered to keep her company during the yuletide festivities. She hadn't asked the favor of him.

"With your permission, Mrs. Penford, I shall find seats for Miss Penford and myself." He flashed his rakish grin, and Aubriella's heart flip-flopped in her chest.

"There. See, Minnie?" Her relief apparent, Mama patted Jessamine's arm. "It has all worked out."

Jessamine mouthed, "I'm sorry," before permitting their mother to tow her away like a barge.

When had Jessamine grown up and begun considering others' feelings?

"Does that happen often?" Jack's question was too casual, too nonchalant.

Aubriella despised his pity.

She slanted him a sharp look.

"What do you think? Surely, you've observed our familial interactions long enough to know the answer." She hitched a shoulder as she searched for a table with room for them. "I'm accustomed to it and do rather well on my own."

She shouldn't have to, but she'd learned to manage.

He made a harsh sound in the back of his throat that Aubriella couldn't interpret.

Of course, he appeared utterly splendid, tempting masculinity wrapped in a muscle straining bottle-green jacket and black pantaloons. His emerald cravat pin twinkled playfully. She couldn't remember another time he'd worn such an adornment.

In recent days, she'd observed all manner of details about Jackson Hart Callen Matherfield that had previously gone unnoticed.

Why, she could not fathom.

His brother, Duncan, seated with the Fitzlloyds, waved them over. Jack leaned down as they wended through the tables and whispered, "I have to return to London for a couple of days. Something urgent requires my presence."

Jerking her head upward, Aubriella searched his face's hard contours and angles.

Already a trifle trampled, her bruised emotions

surged forward with a tsunami's force. Temper unbridled and uncontrolled, she snapped, "So you don't have to model for me? Less than four and twenty hours since I won our bet, and you're breaking your word already?"

Aloofness entered his hazel eyes, turning them flintlike.

Ah, here was the ruthless, sardonic businessman others whispered about who'd clawed and scrambled his way to success and wealth. "That's not the reason, though I confess I am relieved. I should be back in three days, and we'll discuss our arrangement then."

Arrangement?

They had a deal.

Aubriella would bet her carefully saved nest egg had she been a man, Jack wouldn't consider breaking his word. Foreign, scorching anger surged through her, heating her blood and temper.

He was no different from her family or most of the people here. Everyone thought she wouldn't mind being disregarded, manipulated, or lied to.

Well, he was wrong.

They were all bloody wrong.

Aware of how easily someone might overhear them, she modulated her tone. "Either you are a man of your word, Jackson Matherfield, or you are not. I won our wager, fair and square."

He narrowed his eyes as he directed her toward an unoccupied corner behind a trio of huge potted elephant ears.

"And had I won, Aubriella, would you have honored your stake?"

Aubriella averted her gaze. "It's not that simple."

"Exactly." Sarcasm he generally reserved for others lanced her.

She'd been naive to believe anything had changed between them.

"My appetite has flown." She lifted her chin and retreated a step. Icy politesse replaced their former friendship. "I'm returning to the house."

"Suit yourself." Without another word, Jack turned his back and made for his brother's table.

With an odd aching in her throat and heart, Aubriella slipped out the door. As she turned to latch the handle, she perused the conservatory. Engaged in conversation and tea, not a single person noted her departure.

In truth, she could disappear, and days would pass before anyone noticed her absence.

Never had she felt more alone, and Jack's impending departure made her realize how much she'd come to rely upon him. She'd been a fool to trust him. An idiot to think this Christmas would differ from a dozen others.

That was what came of banking upon anyone but one's self.

Rebellion, mutiny, and disgust burgeoned within her.

By God, she'd had bloody well enough.

You are not a feckless female, Aubriella Kendra Larkspur Penford.

If you're discontent, do something about it.

I shall!

Suddenly resolute, Aubriella marched to the house, relishing the jarring cold snowflakes hitting her face. She didn't wait for Fredericks, the butler, to open the door but let herself in. Finding the foyer empty, she brushed snow from her cheeks, then stripped off her gloves.

A plump maid humming to herself wandered down the corridor and gave a startled jump when she saw Aubriella. "Did you need something, Miss?"

"Indeed." Aubriella sucked in a breath, bracing herself

for what she was about to do. "Have the Penford coach brought around in fifteen minutes."

THIRTEEN

A half dozen awkward seconds later

AUBRIELLA WOULD SWITCH the conveyance for a mail coach in Westerham, so Mosely didn't have to suffer in the snow. She'd only brought a small purse but would collect her savings from her room in London. As long as the *Ladies of Opportunity* continued their secret betting, she'd have an income to rely upon.

"Of course, miss." The maid gave her a puzzled glance, but nodded and retreated in the direction she'd come.

After taking the stairs two at a time, Aubriella raced to her bedchamber as if the hounds of hell nipped her heels. The need to escape, to flee, so overwhelmed her she trembled. Excitement and anticipation dueled with fear and apprehension about what she was about to do—the adventure she was about to embark upon.

It's about time, her soul sang.

No, it was long, *long* overdue.

She'd either gone stark raving mad or finally found the courage to spread her wings.

Shoving her chamber door open, she all but ran inside.

Roxina, sitting in an armchair with her hair spilling around her shoulders, gasped and jerked her head upward.

"Whatever is the matter, Aubriella?"

"Let's leave. Now. I've already ordered the coach brought 'round to take me to the village. From there, I'll hire a mail coach to London." That would also put anyone inclined to follow off her trail.

Not that anyone would notice her absence.

Naturally, Mosely, bless his loyal heart, would feel the need to inform Papa of her abrupt departure.

Who knew what Aubriella's father would do?

Anything?

Aubriella threw the wardrobe open. "What say you, Zina?"

Roxina was on her feet before Aubriella finished speaking.

"Yes, Elli." She gave an eager nod and swiftly began gathering her clothing. She paused, a mended stocking dangling from one hand. "You should know that Tellinger is selling my house—well, not exactly selling it. Using it as collateral against a loan."

Hairbrush midair, Aubriella paused and half-turned. "He's *what*?"

She couldn't prevent the slight, appalled shriek on the last syllable.

That was why Roxina was in the state she was in.

"Mitchel mortgaged the house to the hilt and defaulted on the loan. Shelby bought the mortgage six years ago so I would have a place to live." She sighed, her shoulders sagging. "But recently, Mitchel impersonated Shelby and borrowed a thousand pounds from nefarious fiends."

"Oh my, Lord." Aubriella felt sick for her friend. "What a vile, unconscionable fiend to put his sister in such jeopardy."

Roxina swiped a tendril of dark hair off her pale cheek.

"Now Shelby has to use the house as security." She stared blankly out the window, where snow continued to filter from the sky. "I've nowhere to go."

Aubriella dropped her hairbrush into her satchel and unceremoniously plopped the other dressing table contents into the bag with alacrity.

"You most certainly do, too. You shall live with me." She grabbed Roxina's hand. "We're going to my Aunt Astrid's. She left her house to me, and it's far past time I took my life into my own hands. I've never fit in with my family. They won't even miss me. In point of fact, I think they'll be relieved to see the last of me."

Sadly, that was true.

"What about the *Ladies of Opportunity*?" Roxina shoved clothing into her small bag before hurrying to the dressing table. She wound her shiny locks into a simple knot, securing it with a few pins. "I confess, I rely upon that income. It is my sole source of funds at present. Mitchel stopped providing household funds months ago. Now I know why."

"The *Ladies of Opportunity* shall continue as we have always done." Aubriella also depended upon the income and would now, more than ever. "Of course, we'll have to find a new location for our meetings and journey to London to attend them, but it's only ten miles from Aunt Astrid's. Perhaps, we shall expand our ventures. Discreetly, of course."

Roxina pulled her winged brows together. "I'll need to go to the house to pack my personal things."

Aubriella needed to collect a few items herself, including da Vinci's drawings.

Face ravaged with grief, Roxina swallowed and knuckled away a tear. "Shelby's also using the furnishings to repay Mitchel's debt. Not that the out of fashion, worn out furniture will bring much coin."

"God rot Shelby Tellinger for an unscrupulous, self-serving cad." Aubriella glanced around, double-checking that she'd packed all her belongings before crossing to the bell pull.

"He had no choice, Aubriella." Roxina fastened the threadbare frogs of her cloak.

Roxina, defending her nemesis, brought Aubriella up short. "How so?"

"Mitchel borrowed money from dangerous men." Roxina slipped her shoes on. "Shelby doesn't have the cash to repay them. He didn't say as much, but I believe they threatened him. He's as much a victim as I am."

Eyebrows arched in disbelief, Aubriella snorted. "*Pshaw*. What tripe. Men are never as desperate as women. Did he mention selling *his* house or using it as collateral?"

Mouth parted, Roxina stared at her. "No. He did not."

"There you have it." Aubriella pursed her lips, still frothing with frustration. "The inarguable truth is, men simply cannot be trusted. I won a wager last night, and Jackson Matherfield has already reneged. Without a jot of compunction or remorse, I might add. Had I been a man, I doubt he would've dared such blatant disregard."

Roxina crossed to her and took her hand. "I trust you'll tell me about this mysterious private wager on the way?"

"I shall." Aubriella gave a distracted nod. "We need to hurry, however. The snow increases, Zina, and we must stop in London before continuing to Aunt Astrid's. Once in Town, I intend to hire a hack to take us the distance, so pack sparingly."

Roxina snorted this time. "Have no fear there. I own little."

Aubriella's heart pinched with sympathy, but Roxina was as proud as Aubriella and despised any show of pity.

Roxina laughed, a sad, hollow-sounding warble, despite her intrepidness.

"Let's swear off men, dear friend." She linked her arm with Aubriella's. "And vow to remain spinsters. We'll steer the ships of our lives and disdain the winds of fate, society, and men filling our sails to control us."

"Indeed." A wave of sadness sluiced through Aubriella. For a few days, Jack had ensured she wasn't treated as an invisible wallflower. He'd even kissed her as if he truly desired her. With a ragged sigh, she shoved her ruminations into a moldering closet and locked the door. "Who needs men, anyway?"

What she experienced this past week would have to be enough. Yet even as she made her way below with Roxina, Aubriella knew it never would be.

FOURTEEN

Stockworth Manor – Drawing room

HOLDING A GLASS OF CLARET, Jack stood beside the blazing fire and examined the cheerful tableau before him. Festive ribbon-adorned greeneries now festooned the drawing, entry, ballroom, and dining rooms. Laughing guests, swathed in evening finery and dripping with glittering jewels, milled about.

So far, the Templetons' yuletide house party was a rousing success.

The Penfords had entered the drawing room fifteen minutes ago, Lenora Langford and her husband, Stephen, five minutes later. Though Emmet hobbled around with a borrowed cane, he hadn't stopped grinning since arriving.

The only thing missing to complete the evening was Aubriella's pretty face, her ready—often droll—wit, and her perceptive acumen.

94

Would she remain in her chamber for supper too?

People had commented on her and Roxina Danforth's absence this afternoon.

Jack missed Aubriella's company, but understood she needed time to process her disappointment. It wasn't like her to pout, though he knew he'd made her angry. Rather than seek her out to explain there'd been a fire at one of his restaurants, he'd decided to let her temper cool. Though grateful for the temporary respite in having to honor his wager with her, he couldn't help but worry about the restaurant.

Thank God all the staff and patrons had escaped without harm. According to the letter sent by the manager and delivered by special messenger just before tea today, the staff contained the fire damage to the kitchen. Still, the smoke had permeated and damaged the dining area, too.

He needed to inspect the building to determine if he'd rebuild, move the restaurant to a new location, or abandon the venture altogether. He and Duncan had considered opening a seashore inn and restaurant in Brighton or Bath—mayhap now was the time to do so.

He took a sip of wine and returned Emmet's nod of greeting.

While waiting for the dinner gong to sound, the guests assembled for a pre-dinner drink and conversation. The snow continued to fall outside, although not with the intensity it had earlier today. Five or six inches had accumulated, and as long as it didn't snow heavily overnight, he could leave tomorrow as planned.

He'd ride rather than take a coach. It was faster and easier to maneuver. Deucedly colder, too. If all went well, he should return in three days, just as he promised Aubriella.

A commotion at the door drew his attention.

Fredericks, the Templetons' staid-as-a-corpse butler, crossed the room with such alacrity several guests turned to watch his progress. Without preamble, he spoke near Mr. Penford's ear.

Mr. Penford gawped at the butler, then blinked behind his thick spectacles as if he couldn't comprehend what he'd heard.

Fredericks said something further and discreetly gestured toward the doorway.

Mr. Penford touched his wife's shoulder and whispered in her ear. Her expression confused, Mrs. Penford finally dragged her attention from their youngest child, preening before a trio of young bucks.

One hand linked through her husband's elbow, Mrs. Penford grasped Jessamine's hand and all but hauled her toward the exit.

Noticing something was afoot, Emmet, leaning heavily on his borrowed cane, maneuvered through the crowd toward his parents. His flustered father spoke swiftly and rather frantically as they moved toward the corridor.

Jack set his half-full glass on the mantel.

Across the room, he met Shelby Tellinger's mystified gaze.

Tellinger arched an eyebrow as he gave the Penfords and Langfords, now moving *en masse* toward the exit, a questioning look.

Angling his head and jerking his chin, Jack indicated he meant to follow.

Shelby joined him at the doorway. "Until tonight, I've never seen Clarence Penford anything but sedate and befuddled."

"Neither have I." Jack gave a brief glance over his shoulder as he stepped into the corridor.

Several guests noticed the Penfords' and Langfords' sudden departure, and a buzz of conjecture soon filled the drawing room.

Jack unabashedly followed the family into the dining room.

Mrs. Templeton sat in a chair before the beautifully set table, dabbing her face with a handkerchief while her husband awkwardly patted her shoulder.

"There, there, dumpling," George Templeton soothed. "All will be well."

Would it?

Jack wasn't nearly as confident as Templeton, and he didn't know what was afoot yet.

As Jack approached, remorse and chagrin twisted the coachman's face.

"I tried to dissuade Miss Penford," Mosely said. "But she and Miss Danforth were determined to leave immediately. She was most adamant and said they would go on foot if I didn't take them into Westerham at once. I couldn't let them walk in the snow or chance them coming upon riffraff."

"This will help steady you." Fredericks shoved a glass of brandy into the trembling servant's hand.

From cold or upset?

Likely both.

"And you didn't think to leave a note, man?" Mr. Penford put forth the logical question, his tone the most heated and firm Jack could ever recall of the timid fellow. This was the first time Jack had seen the renowned solicitor in action.

"There wasn't time." Mosely gulped the tumbler's contents. "You know how stubborn Miss Penford can be when she gets a notion."

Aye, when Aubrie dug in her heels, she became positively mulish.

Without being asked to, Fredericks refilled Mosely's glass.

Jack and Shelby drifted closer, unnoticed by the room's other occupants.

After taking another healthy gulp, Mosely bobbed his wizened head, his ears still glowing red from the cold. "I would've returned hours ago to alert you, but the coach slid off the track a few miles back. The roads are a wreck. No one's traveled over them yet. It took me some time to realize I couldn't free the coach. I had to unhitch the team and walk back with them."

"I'll send a few stout fellows and a new team to retrieve the coach," Templeton offered while continuing to comfort his distraught wife.

"But where is Aubriella?" Mrs. Penford finally found her voice, sounding genuinely concerned. "I cannot believe my most sensible child would do something so imprudent. I never have to fuss about her."

"She and Miss Danforth boarded the mail coach to London. I tried to dissuade her." Mosely hung his head, the picture of dejection and penitence. He swallowed, and unshed tears glistened in his eyes when he raised his gaze. "She was in a right awful state. I've never seen her so distraught."

Jack could imagine the mutinous jutting of her chin, the set angle of her jaw, and the sparks of rebellion shining in her eyes. Something about this afternoon— mayhap him telling her he was leaving—had compelled her to toss her normal common sense to the wind.

"At least she made for London," Penford interjected. "That was sensible of her."

Jack glared at the man, the urge to shake some sense into the oblivious fellow so strong he fisted his hands.

Lenora Langford wrapped an arm around her now weeping mother. "Don't trouble yourself, Mama.

Aubriella shall be fine. Don't you always say that? You needn't worry about her because she's the logical, levelheaded child amongst us?"

"Even logical, levelheaded children need their family's attention and love." Jack's thoughts tumbled out his mouth without forethought.

Several appalled gazes riveted on him.

Good.

It was long past time someone spoke directly to the Penfords about their neglect.

"I beg your pardon?" Mr. Penford bristled like a cock of the roost. "Are you implying we don't love Aubriella?"

Jack plowed a hand through his hair. "No. I'm saying you ignore her. Disregard her and are indifferent to her. She's practically invisible to you." He met Penford's confused gaze. "She has said as much to me."

"That cannot be true." Mrs. Penford shook her golden head, her ruby earrings swaying with her intensity. "She is… Well, she's Aubriella." As if that explained everything and nothing more needed saying. "She doesn't need us—"

"You're wrong, Mama," Jessamine piped in, drawing the family's attention.

Brave imp.

"Whatever do you mean, child?" Confusion etched Penford's thin features.

The man was dense as a turnip—obtuse as a rock.

Aubriella obviously didn't inherit her intelligence from her parents.

Jessamine squared her shoulders and thrust her dainty chin upward. "I've seen the hurt in her eyes. We take her for granted. You did it this afternoon at tea." She made a sweeping motion with her hand to include her entire family. "We all sat together, and you were bothered that you might have to move a chair to accommodate Aubriella. She doesn't feel loved or that she is part of our family."

That flighty Jessamine had also noticed what Jack had observed, suggested perhaps there was more to the youngest Penford than a pretty face.

"I… I… I didn't realize." Mrs. Penford wept freely, a handkerchief pressed to her eyes. "My poor, dear girl."

Mr. Penford's throat worked, and he turned away to lift his spectacles and dry his eyes.

"You don't include Elli." Emmet, his hands thrust into his pockets, paced back and forth. Accusation colored his tone. "I've seen it and should have said something sooner. I am just as guilty. How often, Mama and Papa, have you said Aubriella doesn't need attention and guidance? That she would be all right? That you don't worry about her?"

"Clearly, Aubriella is *not* all right. Or else she wouldn't have fled during a snowstorm." Jack strode forward, guilt at his contribution to her flight making his words terse and gnawing at his gut.

It occurred to him that Clarence Penford had no idea what to do.

Someone needed to take charge.

"Exactly how long ago did you leave Miss Penford in Westerham, Mosely?" Jack glanced at the longcase clock situated in a corner. Nearly seven. He'd last seen Aubriella at three. Four hours' head start. In this weather, he could overtake a slow-moving coach easily.

"Around half four, Mr. Matherfield," Mosely said.

He caught Tellinger's attention. "Can you be ready to ride in ten minutes?"

"I'll meet you at the stable." Tellinger headed toward the door.

"You have a firearm with you?" Tellinger never

traveled unarmed, and he likely had multiple weapons at his disposal.

Tellinger gave a terse nod before leaving the room.

"Jack?" Emmet wobbled forward. "I wish I could accompany you, but I would only slow you down. Please bring my sister back safely."

"I have every intention of doing so, my friend." He patted Emmet's shoulder.

"Mr. Templeton?" Jack mentally calculated the distance they'd need to travel and the route to take. "May I impose upon you to have horses saddled? Sturdy horses. Perhaps a bag with extra blankets, too?"

"Of course." Templeton waved at Fredericks. "See to it at once."

"Yes, sir." Fredericks put aside his usual staid dignity and departed the room at an impressive sprint.

Jack pivoted to go, his stomach in knots and fear creeping along his spine.

Two pretty women traveling alone in this weather…

God.

His stomach roiled so violently he couldn't finish the thought.

"Jack?" He faced Mr. Penford.

"Yes?"

"Find Aubriella. Please." Mr. Penford blew his nose noisily.

Mrs. Penford lifted her blotchy face from her saturated hankie. "Yes, Jack. Do. Please. She must know how much we love her. We've been remiss, but we must tell her how sorry we are and ask her forgiveness."

It was on the tip of his tongue to blurt that Aubriella mightn't be in this perilous predicament if they'd told her sooner how they felt when the truth hit him with the force of a bludgeon to the skull.

His gait faltered, and dizziness befuddled his mind for a second.

Jack *loved* Aubriella.

Oh, God. I love her.

Only he hadn't recognized the feelings for what they were. He had loved Aubriella for so long it had become second nature. He adored her uniqueness, quirkiness, freckles, hazel eyes, long limbs, and intelligence. In truth, he cherished her stubbornness, skepticism, prickliness when he teased her, and everything else about her.

And the sooner he had his arse in the saddle, the sooner he could tell her just that.

Please, Lord. Keep her safe.

He rushed from the room, the desire to find her, to make sure she was safe, more important than breathing.

I'm coming, my darling. I'm coming.

FIFTEEN

Boots and Crow Hostelry
A dismal stretch of road between Westerham and
London

Q*UARTER past ten in the evening*

H*UDDLED BESIDE* R*OXINA ON A HARD*, gouged, and scratched wooden bench beneath a grimy, cobweb-strewn window, Aubriella covertly surveyed the Boots and Crow common room. This far from the insipid fire struggling to cast its meager light and heat beyond the soot-entrenched hearth, the cold seeped into her bones from the flimsy wall behind her.

The other mail coach patrons also clustered as near to the insufficient flames as possible, which was to say, several feet away. Other conveyances, two in the last hour, had sought refuge in the small, rundown inn, and those passengers—some quite unsavory—had settled in for the night. By the time the mail coach limped into the slushy courtyard two hours ago, other guests had claimed the hostelry's private chambers.

A broken wheel and lame horse sent the coach drivers to the only nearby lodgings. Once they learned nobody could repair the wheel until tomorrow and neither was there a replacement for the lame horse, they'd comforted themselves with tall mugs of dark ale.

Roxina slipped her hand into Aubriella's and gave a soft squeeze. Leaning close, she whispered, "I don't like the way those men are looking at us."

Aubriella didn't need to ask which men.

An unkempt, bearded pair repeatedly turned their drunken attention toward the women. God only knew how long they had lingered at the corner table, downing bottle after bottle of spirits. Boisterous, crude, and inebriated, they harassed the overworked barmaid, mocked the more refined gentlemen, and unabashedly ogled the women.

Their ribald jokes and coarse language brought blushes to more than one woman's cheeks and earned glowers from the men, although no one dared to tell the ruffians to mind their manners or shut their mouths.

Aubriella and Roxina could either take refuge in the crowded and smoky common room, reeking of garlic, boiled cabbage, unwashed bodies, stale ale, and a sweet, foul unidentifiable odor or stay in the coach overnight. At least inside the shambles of a building, she and Roxina were at less risk of freezing to death.

Ravishment, on the other hand?

That might've been a real possibility if there weren't so many other patrons sprawled about the taproom. In truth, Aubriella wasn't certain she and Roxina were safe. Those foul brutes ogling her didn't seem the type to bother with laws. One wretch, sporting a jagged scar from his eye to where it disappeared into his grungy beard, winked at her and smiled, exposing rotten teeth.

Aubriella averted her gaze, and he guffawed.

Swallowing her fright, she took stock of their situation.

They only needed to get through the night, and they'd be on their way first thing in the morning. Westerham was a mere twenty miles from London. Surely, they'd traveled half that distance today. As long as the roads were passable and no other mishaps befell them, she and Roxina should make London tomorrow midmorning.

She flattened her hand over her churning belly. Her reticule formed a lump where she'd pinned it to her chemise before boarding the coach. Thank God she'd had the foresight to do so. Her gown and cloak draped over her redingote hid the bulge, but given the unsavory characters dispersed around the shabby establishment, fear still tiptoed up and down her spine.

In hindsight, she oughtn't to have departed Mabel and George's in such haste. A day or two more wouldn't have made that much difference to her newly hatched scheme for independence.

In truth, staying and secluding herself would have given her time to plan her escape and future. Unlike her carefully thought out and enacted scheme to sneak into university, for the first time in her life, she'd succumbed to an imprudent, emotional impulse, and now her impetuosity had also endangered her dearest friend.

Lifting her nose and presenting her profile to the obnoxious duo, who continued to leer at her and Roxina, she bit her lip. This unexpected and unfortunate delay in their journey not only put them in an untenable situation, it might prevent their escape to Aunt Astrid's.

Mayhap, as Aubriella often vanished for hours at

house parties, no one would question her absence tonight or tomorrow.

That still left her to get through the night unaccosted.

She'd refused food and drink because there was no way in Hades that she would reveal she possessed a few coins. She wouldn't put it past the assembled riffraff to rob her in her sleep. Which was why she had no intention of sleeping, or at the very least, she and Roxina would slumber in shifts.

"I'm sorry, Zina."

Despite her exhaustion and anxiety, Roxina gave her a sharp look. "Whatever for?"

"For dragging you into my muddle." Aubriella spread a hand to indicate their surroundings. "For this. For not at least asking the cook for a piece of cheese and bread. An apple or two."

"Fiddlesticks and flimflam." Roxina squeezed her hand again. "I have a mind of my own. No one could've known the weather would wreak havoc on the roads, that the coach wheel would need repairing, or that one horse would go lame. Though I'm not surprised, considering the poor beast had to pull the laden coach through thick snow."

Everything she said was true, but that didn't ease Aubriella's guilt.

Roxina marshaled a smile and changed the subject. "I bet Jack was fit to be tied when you won the wager."

"I should have known he never intended to honor it." Closing her eyes, Aubriella leaned her head back, the motion pushing her bonnet forward. This unforeseen delay gave her time to ponder her future and the *Ladies of Opportunity*.

And to think about Jack.

His handsome face had invaded her mind the second she'd lowered her eyelids.

When had her feelings transferred from irritation and annoyance to something much warmer? Much more dangerous to her heart? She'd never had to guard herself against affection before, and perhaps that was why the wily emotion had sneaked up on her.

What she felt for Jack Matherfield most assuredly was not aggravation or exasperation.

But that didn't matter.

Not anymore.

Smelling the odoriferous man before he spoke and swallowing a gag, she opened her eyes. He stood a mere two feet in front of her and Roxina.

Lord, above.

When was the last time he'd bathed or donned clean clothing?

A sloppy, drunken grin splitting his unwashed face and bits of food embedded in his crusty beard, he asked, "Would you pretty lad-dees care to join me an' me friend?" He veered his attention to his table, where his eager chum regarded them with unconcealed lust. "We couldn't help but notice you 'aven't eaten. We'd be happy t' share our meal."

Hell would freeze over first.

"No, thank you, but your kindness is appreciated." Aubriella kept her tone coolly pleasant as she forced the insincere words past her lips. She fashioned a small smile. Who knew what might set this blighter off? "We're waiting for someone. They've been delayed." She waved her hand toward the dusty window. "The inclement weather, you know."

Taking Aubriella's cue, Roxina nodded and squinted into the darkness beyond the dirty windowpane. Snow pelted the glass, which didn't portend well for an early morning departure. "Indeed. They should have arrived by now."

A sinister sneer replaced his buffoonish grin.

"There ain't no one meetin' you. You were on the mail coach." He loomed over them, hands fisted at his hips. "You think yer too good fer us, uppity wenches?"

Resisting the urge to lick her lower lip, Aubriella scanned the faces of the patrons, nearly all staring in her direction. Not a single person, including the innkeeper, could hold her gaze.

Cowards, the lot.

Heart pounding, Aubriella shrank against the wall as the brute reached for her. Unexpectedly, his eyes rounded in astonishment. He dropped his hand to his side, remaining motionless.

Jack stepped from behind his broad back, a pistol in one hand and a blade pressed against the cur's bull-like neck. "She told you she was waiting for someone. We've arrived."

Standing in the center of the taproom, apparently not the least bothered that he pointed a pistol at the other infuriated sod, Shelby Tellinger winked at the barmaid. "Be a love and bring a pot of tea, bread, cheese, and whatever else you have on hand that's fresh and vermin free."

He waved the pistol toward the other lout. "The Cowen brothers were just leaving, and we'll take their table."

How did Shelby know who they were?

The frazzled barmaid gave a cautious nod before disappearing into the kitchen.

Not a single patron moved, their focus fixated on the scene playing out before them.

"The 'ell we are." The miscreant half-rose, but Shelby pointed the gun at the bounder's face, and he slowly lowered himself into his chair again.

"Did I fail to mention my name.?" A lethal tone

Aubriella had never heard laced his voice. "Tellinger. Shelby Tellinger."

The transformation in the men, including the blackguard Jack held at knifepoint, would've been comical if Aubriella could have drawn a breath to laugh. Truth be told, terror riveted her to the bench and stalled her breathing. On the other hand, her pulse raced faster than a horse competing in the Royal Ascot.

Evidently, the troublemakers knew something Aubriella did not, for they wasted no time tossing a few coins on the table and skulking from the inn despite the snowfall.

Why had the men reacted the way they had to Shelby?

She slid a gaze to Roxina, staring at Shelby as if he had two heads from which sprouted four scarlet horns. Grinning, Shelby sank onto one of the newly vacated chairs and sent his flinty gaze around the common room. He waved a hand. "As you were."

The weary patrons went back to their activities, most behaving as if nothing remarkable had just occurred.

Jack didn't tear his gaze from the duo until the door closed. He crossed his arms and stared at Aubriella, his expression inscrutable. "We are going to warm ourselves and eat, ladies. Then we are leaving. The horses should have rested enough by then. Understood?"

Aubriella opened her mouth to argue, but the thunderous look in Jack's hazel eyes made her snap her mouth shut. He extended his hands and helped them up. He released Roxina as soon as she stood, but held Aubriella immobile as Roxina crossed to the table and sat.

The serving wench returned with a laden platter. She placed a stretcher with sliced brown bread, cheese, and what appeared to be meat pies on the scarred tabletop. A teapot and chipped teacups followed.

Jack turned his back to the curious travelers. "You shall have the entire ride, seated before me on a horse, Aubrie, to explain your idiotic behavior."

"I owe you no explanation, Jack." He wasn't her keeper, even if he had rescued her. "Besides, don't you have *urgent* business in London that demands your attention?"

"I do, and that is why we are not returning to the Templetons but continuing to London tonight." Jack flared his nostrils, and his cheekbones stood out as harshness contorted the planes of his face. "I am barely keeping my temper under control. You and Roxina were on the verge of being ravished. Your stupidity not only endangered you, but your friend. For once in your life, do not argue with me, or so help me God, I shall find an empty room and paddle your bottom."

Aubriella couldn't prevent her jaw from sagging.

How dare he?

Who did he think he was?

She wasn't a child he could take to task and spank.

"You wouldn't dare." She tilted her chin in defiance. "Besides, there are no vacant rooms."

He gripped her chin between his thumb and forefinger.

"Do. Not. Push me, Aubriella. I am at the end of my tether." His expression softened, and he caressed her cheek. "I was terrified for you, and I blamed myself for your leaving. If anything had happened to you…"

He closed his eyes, his features etched in agony—as if he truly cared.

For once, Aubriella didn't have a cutting riposte. For as long as she lived, she'd remember his face at that moment. And when he opened his eyes, her soul quivered from the desolation shining there.

SIXTEEN

Outside London

THREE HOURS LATER – 21 DECEMBER

JACK GLANCED DOWN AT AUBRIELLA, fast asleep in his arms. The snow had stopped half an hour after they departed the inn. Though teeth-cracking cold outside, the journey hadn't been as arduous as he'd expected. That was due, in part, to the Flemish horses Templeton had provided. Larger and stronger than typical horses, their endurance matched their big, gentle hearts.

Unnaturally subdued, Aubriella had eaten, and after he'd arranged for the mail coach drivers to deliver her and Miss Danforth's luggage, she'd meekly allowed Jack to lift her onto his mount. His gun at his waist, he climbed into the saddle, then wrapped them both in the extra blankets Templeton had sent.

Across the circular courtyard, Tellinger did the same with Miss Danforth.

Both women had fallen asleep within minutes, and

more than once on the trek to London, he'd caught Tellinger watching Miss Danforth just as Jack observed Aubriella.

Were his feelings as transparent as Tellinger's?

Apparently not to the women they loved, who disdained them at every turn.

In a few minutes, Jack would awaken Aubriella. He had things he needed to say and would have her word that she wouldn't pelt off again without telling him. Skimming his gaze over her winged eyebrows, the delicate flare of her sweet lips, and the slope of her cheeks, his heart swelled with love.

How could he not have known he loved her?

God above, when he'd entered the Boot and Crow and seen that behemoth looming over her, her face waxen and fraught with fright, Jack had wanted to kill the bloody cur. He'd also wanted to spank her for terrifying him by leaving without telling anyone and then kiss her tears away while begging her forgiveness for hurting her.

Instinct told him to tread cautiously when declaring himself to Aubriella. She probably wouldn't believe him. His heart ached for her. She'd erected such a wall of protection around herself that he'd have to use all his wit and skill to tear down the ramparts.

Truth be told, Jack wasn't certain he of his success, but by thunder, he would try.

She stirred as if sensing he gazed at her, and her eyelids fluttered open. It was impossible to read her expression in the dark, but he thought a smile might've bent her mouth.

"How long have I slept?" She yawned delicately behind her hand.

"About two hours, I think." The fresh snow had made progress slow. He adjusted her on his lap so she sat more upright and gritted his teeth against the sensual onslaught the movement caused. "We are near London. You can see the lights in the distance. You should be home, tucked into your bed within the hour."

An owl hooted, breaking the night's stillness interrupted only by the plodding horses' footsteps.

"Thank you, Jack." Huskiness tinged her voice. "I don't know what…"

"*Shh.*" *My darling.* "You are safe now." *And I intend that you always shall be.* Somehow, he must convince her of his love, and she must marry him.

"Why did you come after me?" She cupped his jaw with her gloved hand, and his heart swelled to bursting.

He barely resisted the urge to turn his head and press his lips into her palm. On the verge of declaring himself, he swallowed his vows of adoration and love. When he told Aubriella of his affection, it wouldn't be while freezing atop a horse in the middle of the night when he couldn't see her reaction.

Instead, he murmured, "With Emmet injured, I was the most logical person. Besides, I had to return to London. No sense disrupting the other house guests' revelries."

"Yes, I suppose you are right." She angled her face away, but Jack would've sworn disappointment leached into her voice. "I'm sorry to be an inconvenience and to have detained you from your business."

STUPID, senseless tears stung behind Aubriella's eyes.

For a few timeless seconds, she'd thought Jack meant to say something entirely different. Lord, she'd wanted him to say something to convince her not to move to Aunt Astrid's house. To persuade her that what Aubriella felt for him wasn't one-sided—that she wouldn't live out her days alone and misunderstood. An oddity who people whispered about behind hands and fans.

More fool her.

She craned her neck to see how Roxina fared.

Her friend still slept, slumped against Shelby's chest.

Aubriella narrowed her eyes.

"How did Shelby know who the Cowen brothers were?" She didn't bother facing Jack, since it was impossible to see his face. His heat warmed her back, beckoning her to lean against his solid strength, and his ironlike arm across her waist comforted her.

Jack stiffened for an instant, but after exhaling, he relaxed against her. "If I don't tell you, you'll simply ask him, won't you?"

A reluctant grin tipped the corners of her mouth upward.

Jack knew her so well.

Better than anyone else, other than Roxina. "I shall."

If only he could love her.

"There are many facets about Tellinger that he keeps private." Jack's thighs flexed beneath her bottom as the arm around her waist tightened minutely. "One of which is that he is a bounty hunter on occasion. A very good bounty hunter, and that is why the Cowens tucked their tails and fled. He'd likely seen their wanted posters. I've little doubt that he would have attempted to bring them in if you and Roxina hadn't been present."

"You don't say?" Aubriella stretched her neck again to catch a glimpse of Shelby speaking in low tones to Roxina. "He doesn't look like what I imagine a bounty hunter would look like. Not rough and burly and threatening."

Jack chuckled, the warm resonance causing an

answering peal in her heart. "It's cliché, but appearances can be deceiving."

"My da Vinci drawings are of human dissections." Aubriella wasn't sure why she blurted that secret to Jack. Perhaps to see his reaction. Mayhap because she wanted to share something so important with another person, and he was the only one who might understand her fascination with the human form.

Another chuckle vibrated his chest before he pulled her closer, and this time, she distinctly felt him nuzzle the back of her head through her bonnet.

A tiny seed of hope took root.

"You are the most fascinating, intriguing, remarkable, daring woman."

She wrinkled her nose. Not the romantic declarations she yearned for. "I'm sure you meant those as compliments, Jack, but they make me sound like an eccentric old tabby." She grinned at the image of herself, a wrinkled, bespeckled old prune hunched over naughty drawings. "Which I suppose I am."

"An utterly delightful eccentric." Amusement accented each syllable. "And assuredly *not* an old tabby."

Jack had never disdained or disparaged her unusual interests.

The owl hooted again, or perchance it was another answering the first.

A cow, disturbed from her rest by their passing, mooed a low protest in the nearby meadow. The snow blanketing the fields and covering the houses like icing on pastries gave the landscape a fairytale-like appearance.

"You'll need to pen a letter to your family to let them know you are all right," Jack murmured in her ear, his warm breath causing a delicious little shiver to scuttle across her shoulders. "They were quite frantic."

"That I find hard to believe." Her sarcasm grated harshly in her ears. "That's why I'm moving to the house my Aunt Astrid left me before they return. I'm tired of being an outsider—a misunderstood peculiarity—in my own home."

That plan had not changed, despite the unexpected delay.

After resting for a few hours, Aubriella would pack her most cherished and necessary belongings. If Roxina still wanted to accompany her, they would depart before the sun dipped low on the horizon tomorrow.

"Promise me you won't do anything until I call upon you." Jack squeezed her ribs when she didn't respond. "Please, Aubrie. I must check on the fire damage in one of my restaurants, but as soon as I have done so, I would like to speak with you about an important matter."

Gasping, she gripped his forearm and twisted to look at him.

"Fire? Oh, Jack, that's awful. Was anyone hurt?"

He hadn't been trying to renege on their wager, as she'd believed. Nevertheless, the tragedy gave him an excuse to do just that.

"No one was injured, thank God. But I have to evaluate the extent of the damage." A yawn escaped him. He must be exhausted.

"I don't think there is any reason for me to delay my plans to move, Jack." Neck bent, Aubriella stared at the shadowy landscape. "I've known for a while that I needed to do something different. Get on with my life. Forge a path for myself."

It didn't matter that she didn't know precisely what her future looked like. But that was fine. She could anticipate the journey.

"We can talk about that when I call." Jack nudged her

chin upward, forcing her to meet his eyes in the darkness. "Please promise me, Aubrie."

She hunched a shoulder. "I'll give you until tomorrow afternoon, though I doubt anything you have to say shall change my mind."

Unless it includes a vow of undying love and a marriage proposal.

If only such a marvelous thing were possible.

However, that was as likely as Mitchel Danforth becoming a monk or Francine Willoughby becoming a nun. And Aubriella was too pragmatic to indulge in fanciful dreams that would only lead to a broken heart.

They'd entered the outskirts of London, and a scraggly cat darted across the street. The city's familiar stench surrounded them like heavy fog. Traffic had rid most of the street of thick snow, though the pavement was slick in places, and dirty snow mounds paralleled the lane's sides.

"You have my word, Aubrie. Before the sun sets tomorrow, I shall knock upon your door."

The horse snorted and swished its long tail—poor beast. It was probably just as weary as they were.

She sighed and fiddled with the horse's mane. "I release you from your obligation to pose for me, Jack. I never should've asked that of you."

Why did it feel as if Aubriella were saying goodbye to him, even though she'd vowed to wait a day before leaving? The pain impaling her heart hitched her breath, and she blinked away a fresh wave of stinging tears.

Unrequited love did indeed cleave one's heart in two.

"I still want to know how you came by the information about Francine Willoughby." No humor colored Jack's words now. "I suspect I'll not like the answer."

"That's why I shan't tell you," she quipped with far more light-heartedness than she felt.

He sighed, his breath tickling her neck.

"You still don't trust me, Aubrie?"

How Aubriella wanted to, but she couldn't.

Not with the *Ladies of Opportunity*. That must remain a secret.

Too much was at stake.

SEVENTEEN

Penfords' House, Mayfair—London
ALMOST HALF FIVE **the next afternoon**

JACK BRUSHED a hand over his jacket pocket, where a pearl-cut engagement ring lay tucked inside a crimson velvet box. It had taken longer to conclude his business, follow up on Francine Willoughby, and shop for the ring than he had expected.

Nevertheless, the soft golden glow shining in the Penfords' windows eased the tension in his chest.

Aubriella had kept her word and waited for him.

After Jack's brisk double rap upon the door, Styles, the Penfords' diminutive butler, opened the door. Expression benign and his head barely reaching Jack's shoulder, he stepped aside with the grandeur of a prince. "Mr. Matherfield."

Jack entered, coming up short at the trunks and crates stacked in the foyer on the D'Aremberg patterned parquet floor.

Aubriella had been busy, it seemed.

"Miss Penford's, I presume?" Jack swept his hand toward the stacks.

Alarm mixed with trepidation assailed him.

At least Aubriella hadn't left already, but from the array filling the entry, she fully intended to. And this was no visit. She meant to move for good. That she'd been so unhappy she would leave the bosom of her family made his lungs cramp with empathy for her. She was of age. Legally, there was nothing anyone could do to stop her.

"Indeed, sir." Styles nodded, his expression folding into concerned creases. "She is most determined to vacate the house today." He darted a hasty glance down the corridor before stepping nearer. "I've taken the liberty of sending a message to her parents, but they won't return in time to prevent her departure."

If they returned.

Nonetheless, the Penfords' sincere reactions two nights ago gave Jack hope they truly cared about Aubriella. Besides, the Penfords needn't cut their holiday short if all went well. He and Aubriella would return to Stockworth Manor betrothed. There, they'd celebrate the most marvelous Christmas ever.

Jack cupped the butler's thin shoulder. "I have something that I hope"—*pray*—"will change her mind. Is she in the drawing room or library?"

Naturally, she couldn't receive him in her bedchamber.

Tipping his lips upward a fraction and amusement gleaming in his eyes, Styles said, "The library, sorting through books to take with her."

Of course, she was.

"I know the way." Going over his rehearsed speech one last time, Jack pivoted toward the stairs.

"Shall I request refreshments, Mr. Matherfield?"

Jack paused, then nodded. "Yes, please. Champagne if you have it."

"*Champagne*, sir?" Styles' considerably grizzled eyebrows crawled up his forehead and wriggled there like a pair of great hairy caterpillars in the throes of death. "That's rather celebratory, is it not?"

"I intend to propose to the most remarkable woman alive." Smiling like a giddy idiot, Jack patted his pocket. "Wish me luck."

An unfettered grin split Styles' face. "Champagne it is, and the best of good fortune to you. How long shall I wait?"

Likely, news of Jack's intentions would spread throughout the house within minutes, and the servants would brazenly eavesdrop outside the library door.

"I shall ring for you." Jack continued down the corridor, the confident click of his boot heels echoing with each step. How often had he walked this same path, but never for a reason as important as what brought him to Mayfair today?

He hadn't even considered what he'd do if Aubriella said no to his proposal.

He wouldn't give up. That was for certain.

Persistence and patience.

That was how he'd win her over.

Outside the library, he took a calming breath and wiped his sweaty palms on his trousers.

My God, he'd never been so nervous in his life.

Peeking in the half-open door, he spied Aubriella sitting on the floor, piles of books surrounding her. She wore one of her *work* gowns, as she called them.

She could've worn a beggar's filthy and tattered rags and still would've been the most beautiful woman on earth to him. Her expression a mélange of desolation and resignation, she gazed out the window where the winter breeze caressed a barren dogwood's branches.

Jack slipped into the room, drinking her in. This woman had set up house in his heart, and he couldn't fathom a future without her now.

"Aubrie?"

"The sun set over an hour and a half ago." She didn't turn around. "I thought you weren't coming."

"I'm sorry I'm late. Things just took longer than I anticipated." Yielding to the urgency thrumming through him to be near her, Jack crossed the room, kneeled on one knee, and touched her shoulder.

"Why are you here, Jack?"

She still didn't look at him.

Unease scraped along his spine, but he shrugged it off.

After shoving a stack of books aside, Jack lowered himself to the floor and grazed a finger down her velvety cheek. "Won't you look at me?"

Sighing, she finally met his gaze.

He gave her a tender smile filled with all the love he held for her. "I told you I had something important to discuss with you, darling."

Her gorgeous hazel-green eyes widened at the endearment, and her pretty mouth parted in surprise. Jack's heart soared heavenward at her unconcealed pleasure. Nevertheless, in typical Aubriella fashion, she composed herself in the next blink.

"What is this important matter?" She waved a hand toward the books. "I'm almost done here. I'd intended to leave tonight…"

But she'd waited.

For him.

She didn't need to say it.

Her soft, adoring gaze revealed the truth.

"I love you, Aubriella."

The crackling, spitting fire emphasized the pregnant silence that descended on the room. Several seconds crept by with infinite slowness.

"*What?*" she finally asked breathlessly before skepticism created two lines on her forehead, and bleakness replaced the light in her eyes. "Ah, I see. Back to your old mocking tricks again? I thought we'd put that behind us. More fool me."

"Not a bit of it." Jack took Aubriella's hand and pressed his mouth to her smooth wrist. Her pulse beat a frenetic staccato beneath the skin.

"I adore you, Aubrie. I have loved you for so long. But fool that I am, I didn't realize what I felt was love. I just knew I was happiest when I was with you. You made me smile and brought joy and excitement into my life whenever I was near you."

So much for rehearsed, romantic speeches.

"I thought you felt sorry for me, and that was the only reason you spent time with me." A tremulous, nascent smile bent her mouth.

He cradled her hand in his—no sense lying.

"I did pity you at times. But when you left the Templetons in the snow, I was so afraid for you. It struck me then that what I felt for you was soul-shattering love." He quirked his mouth into a boyish grin. "And I hope that you love me, too. Just a little."

"I do." She laughed, a watery joy-filled warble, and swiped away the lone crystalline tear trailing down her cheek. "I tried to convince myself it was annoyance and irritation, but I finally had to admit I loved you."

Thank God. For a moment there...

Aubriella, who never wept, brushed away another teardrop. "I didn't dare hope that you felt the same, and it nearly killed me to think you'd fathered Francine's child."

"Impossible." If Aubriella was to be his wife, she should know everything about him. "The truth is, I've never been with a woman. My love, I've never wanted to be intimate with anyone except for you."

A tiny gasp escaped her before a radiant smile lit her face.

"*Never*? But you're so handsome, and the way women flock to you." She lifted her shoulder an inch. "I assumed you were a man of the world."

Jack shook his head.

"It's not something I speak of, but the woman I intend to marry should know the truth." Nerves turned his fingers to jelly, and he fumbled in his pocket, finally grasping the burgundy ring box. After extracting the velvety square, he opened the lid and held the twinkling jewel nestled in ivory satin before her.

"Marry me, my darling, Aubrie. You can study the human form as much as you like. I'll buy you copies of every rendering da Vinci ever drew and as many books on anatomy as your heart can stand." He waggled his eyebrows and gave her a devilish grin. "Other less respectable books and drawings I know of might interest you too, and I'd be happy to pose for you sans my clothing."

She released an unfettered giggle, an adorable hint of pink appearing on her cheeks. "My heart doesn't need those things anymore. It has you to fill it now, though I fully intend to draw you, but not naked. Someone might see the sketches, and your body is for my enjoyment alone."

"Indeed." Desire sparked, causing a predictable physical reaction to the unintended erotic images she aroused.

Aubriella lifted the ring from its velvet mooring and slipped it on her finger.

"It's gorgeous," she murmured in awe. "Almost exactly like the one I described to Roxina many years ago when we were still in finishing school and visiting Mabel and George for Christmas."

Jack had been there.

She lifted her misty-eyed gaze to his. "How did you know?"

"I overheard you." Jack pulled Aubriella onto his lap, and she let out a tiny yelp of surprise before settling into his chest like a contented kitten. "Even all those years ago, my heart knew what my mind did not. You are my soulmate."

Eyes glistening, she lifted her mouth to his.

"Kiss me, Jack."

The scintillating sexual current between them, since he'd entered the library, erupted into a full-blown conflagration at her bidding.

Ravenous, he plundered her mouth, stroking her tongue with his even as he caressed her rounded curves. Clutching his shoulders, Aubriella moaned into his mouth. The sound caused a primitive, animalistic growl deep in his throat. Several passionate minutes passed in which he laid her on the floor and covered her body with his, showing her with his mouth how much he loved her.

A sneeze followed by frenetic whispering made him lift his head from nuzzling her delectable bosom.

Quirking an eyebrow, he jerked his chin toward the closed door and whispered, "I think we have eavesdroppers. I might've told Styles I intended to propose and asked him to bring us champagne."

Her eyes flew open and locked with his before veering toward the paneled door. "The servants? Oh, dear."

She slapped her hand over her mouth to stifle her giggles.

Of course, she wouldn't blush from embarrassment.

This was Aubriella, after all.

Jack scooted into a sitting position and then stood. He helped her to her feet, and she tried to tidy her hopelessly mussed hair.

"When you are ready, I'd like to hear about your *secret* enterprise." Jack caressed her cheek. "I suspect Roxina and your other friends are also involved."

"Oh, Jack." Aubriella bit her lower lip, her indecision and apprehension apparent. "If we are to wed, I cannot keep secrets from you." Sighing, she shook her head. "Similar to men's betting books, we hold the bank for bets placed by women. It's to supplement their income, or in some cases, it is their only financial provision."

"A *betting book?*" Jack couldn't keep the astonishment from his voice. "For women?"

She gave a cautious nod.

"We have strict rules about what wagers we accept, who we accept them from, and how the funds are dispersed." She laid her palm against his chest. "For some women like Roxina, they have no other source of income, Jack."

He blew out a breath. Aubriella and her friends ran a gambling ring. "I shan't forbid you to continue with your venture, but I would like to have a discussion and learn the details."

"Of course." Relief washed over her features. "You'd be amazed at our clients and the things I've learned."

"I'm sure I would be." Not entirely happy with this turn of event, Jack set his concerns aside for now. There'd be plenty of time to examine the situation later. He'd just become affianced, and nothing would ruin this occasion.

"Shall we invite the servants in and share our good news?" He encircled her waist and drew her close, speaking into her hair.

"I suppose we must." She tilted her head to look up at him. "Then I want to discuss how quickly we can marry. I quite like that kissing business, and I know there's much more to lovemaking."

"Is my future wife a wanton?" Jack chuckled as he angled them toward the door. "I certainly hope so."

"Perhaps." Aubriella gave him a seductress's smile. "I cannot wait to find out."

EPILOGUE

Stockworth Manor ballroom, Westerham, England

24 December 1818

As the orchestra played the last notes of a minuet, Aubriella extended her hand for inspection the umpteenth time this evening. She and Jack had arrived at Stockworth Manor last night, and news of their betrothal had swept through the guests the next day.

For once, Aubriella could smile proudly and confidently.

A starry-eyed teenager, she'd dreamed of a pear-shaped diamond surrounded by a rectangular halo of smaller diamonds. Jack had found her that exact ring.

As Cousin Mabel examined the glittering ring, she fairly beamed as if she'd personally arranged the match between her niece and Jack. "Well done, my dear. Jackson Matherfield is quite the catch and not hard on the eyes either. I've always known there was a special spark between you two. A wonder it took so long for you to realize it."

Now that Aubriella admitted her love for Jack, she could scarcely believe she'd been blind for so long either. As if compelled by an unseen force that prevented her from exercising her will, she searched the ballroom for her future husband.

Her gaze locked with Jack's across the room, and he kicked his mouth into a mischievous smile as he caressed her with his smoldering gaze.

They'd agreed on a short betrothal and planned to marry in the middle of January.

"It is too bad Miss Danforth and Mr. Tellinger did not return for the festivities," Mabel said a bit too offhandedly. "After all these years, it doesn't seem the same without them or our annual skit. But I didn't see how I could continue with preparations for the performance without Miss Danforth's assistance."

Her cousin's gentle gaze didn't deceive Aubriella.

She was dying to know why, but the secrets weren't for Aubriella to tell.

Roxina had accepted Aubriella's offer to live in Aunt Astrid's house—now Aubriella's. Shelby Tellinger vowed he must locate Mitchel Danforth and sell the Danforths' house. Jack revealed Shelby might need to disappear for a time for his safety. At least until Shelby satisfied his debt with the loan sharks.

"I cannot say the same about the Willoughbys, though." A displeased expression pinched Mabel's mouth, and she pursed her lips. "Never could abide them, but I always extended an invitation for dear George's sake. They left without so much as a by your leave." She huffed out an exasperated breath. "Rest assured. I'll not invite them next year."

According to Jack, Francine had snared herself a doddering, one-foot-in-the-grave vicar and was to exchange wedding vows the day after Christmas. A crony of her father's, Reverend Balthazar Digby, had agreed to wed the chit and claim the child as his, though no one with an iota of common sense would believe the farcical tale.

The substantial purse and annual allowance offered as an enticement likely sealed the deal. The good reverend had a penchant for gambling and hadn't two coins to rub together.

The promise of an annual income must've been too much for a man of the cloth about to retire to resist. Now that Digby was guaranteed a comfortable dotage, with Francine for a wife, he'd probably be claiming several by-blows as his progeny.

Aubriella hadn't asked Jack how he'd come by that information. She'd bet Shelby had something to do with it, however.

Lady Lovegrove must be quite pleased. Not only was she spared her noxious niece's daily company, she'd won a tidy purse because of her wager.

Smiling, Mabel fluttered her fingers toward Winnie Cavender across the room, one of the four unknown siblings Aubriella had first seen at breakfast a few mornings ago. "The Cavenders seem to have fit into our little troupe, haven't they?"

"They have," Aubriella responded automatically, for she observed Jack's progress in her direction beneath her lashes.

The orchestra had struck up a waltz. In all the years she'd known Jack, she'd never danced with him. It didn't matter any longer that she'd probably trod upon his toes and miss a step. As long as he held her in his arms, she was content.

"Excuse me. I see a muddle about to occur." Cousin Mabel squeezed Aubriella's forearm. She trotted off, shooing people out of her way as she sailed forth, as only Mabel could do.

"There you are, dearest." Mama swooped in and bussed Aubriella's cheek. "You're so lovely this evening." Mama gave an approving nod. "I knew that blue would suit you."

Papa pecked her cheek as well. "Enjoying yourself, my pet?"

His use of Aubriella's childhood pet name caused a lump to form in her throat.

Never in memory had her parents been this attentive.

"How could I not?" The ice-blue satin gown trimmed in silver ribbons and its silver-lace overskirt adorned with hundreds of crystals sparkled like a star in the midnight sky. And for the first time at a gathering, Aubriella felt beautiful. "I'm to marry Jack in three weeks."

Emmet, walking better but still using his cane, limped to her side. "I cannot be happier at your news, dear sister. I know no finer man than Jack Matherfield and welcome him as a brother."

To a person, the Penford family was exuberant that Aubriella and Jack would soon march down the aisle. She couldn't quite decide if that was because she'd finally found a husband, or if they were genuinely happy for her. Given the dramatic turnabout in their mannerism and behavior since she'd arrived, she hoped for the latter.

Jack stopped before her and, with that wicked grin she'd come to know meant he entertained thoughts only a soon-to-be-husband was permitted, grasped her fingers and lifted them to his mouth.

After kissing the back of her hand, he tucked it into

the crook of his arm. "Please tell me this dance isn't claimed."

She nearly swatted him.

Not so much had changed that suitors had vied to fill Aubriella's dance card. "I believe I have this dance free."

Jack gave her parents and Emmet a smart bow. "If you'll permit me to abscond with my fiancée?"

"By all means, Jack. Mrs. Penford, might I persuade you to take to the floor?" Papa wrapped an arm around Mama's waist and urged her forward, too.

Mama blushed like a schoolgirl before acquiescing.

"I don't dance well, Jack." Aubriella apologized as they took their positions.

She curtsied, and he bowed.

"That's because you've never had the right partner, my darling Aubrie."

"Or because I have two left feet, each of which is weighted with dried cement," she responded drolly.

Bless Jack for his optimism. Particularly since a mere fortnight ago, he was the most cynical man she knew.

Had love changed him, too?

He swept her into his arms and whisked her across the dance floor. "When you let love guide you, my sweet, nothing else matters."

Then he lowered his mouth to hers, and nothing else did matter.

THE END

I hope you enjoyed
and following Jack and Aubriella's romantic holiday
journey.

If you'd like to leave a review,
I would be so grateful.

Thank you for reading THE WALLFLOWER'S WILD WAGER. Unlike the other series I've written, *Ladies of Opportunity* doesn't feature any lords or ladies as main characters, although they rub elbows with the aristocracy. I wanted this series to stand apart, showing the scope of challenges commoners faced in a time and place that catered to the privileged.

I had to do a bit of research about the dice game, Hazards. With any luck, my facts are accurate, and if I missed a detail or two, I beg for your forgiveness. Though it wasn't exactly *de rigueur*, women of means occasionally operated gambling salons and "held the bank," or controlled the funds. More often, however, the ladies held gaming parties featuring faro and other popular games at their homes. The Ladies of Opportunity engage in a less acceptable and riskier endeavor by modeling their wagering after White's Betting Book, which permitted bets on just about anything, not just cards and dice.

As I'm sure you noticed, I dedicated an entire chapter to Shelby and Roxina, the hero and heroine of the next story in the series, THE SPINSTER'S SECRET STAKES. That was deliberate so you could have a deeper glimpse into them as characters. I shall do the same with books two and three in the series.

You may have also observed that I don't always strictly adhere to British spelling and grammar. That is because, although my book is set in England, most of my readers are American. I am confident my readers on both sides of the pond can adjust to those minor differences.

Whether you're a new reader to my books or a loyal

fan, I hope you enjoyed a peaceful interlude with Jack and Aubriella.

Until next time,
Hugs,
Collette Cameron®

If you haven't joined Collette's exclusive mailing list click on QR image to sign up! You'll get access to exclusive content, sneak peeks, contests, giveaways, and more...

(P.S. No spam!)

https://collettecameronbooks.com/freegift

**Collette loves to hear from readers.
You can contact her via her website:
collettecameronbooks.com.
Or email her directly at
collette@collettecameronbooks.com.**

You can also follow Collette on social media:
Facebook: https://www.-
facebook.com/ColletteCameronNovels/
Instagram:
https://instagram.com/collettecameronauthor/
Goodreads: https://www.-
goodreads.com/collettecameron
Book Bub: https://www.bookbub.com/authors/collette-
cameron

ABOUT THE AUTHOR

COLLETTE CAMERON®

USA Today Bestselling author Collette Cameron® is renowned for her captivating, humorous, and heartwarming Scottish and Regency historical romance novels. With over 65 published titles, over 1.6 million books sold around the world, and multiple writing awards to her credit, Collette is a well-known author in the world of historical romance.

Readers love her witty and relatable characters including daring rogues, dashing scoundrels, and the strong and spirited heroines who capture their hearts. From the rugged highlands to the refined drawing rooms of Regency England, Collette's novels will transport you to another time and place, where love and adventure are just a page away.

Collette's Sweet-to-Spicy Timeless Romances® are the perfect escape for readers looking for romantic escape, poignant inspiration, engaging humor, and entertaining stories.

Based in the Pacific Northwest, Collette is surrounded by the lush greenery and rainy skies that inspire her writing. She dreams of one day splitting her time between the Pacific Northwest and Scotland. In the meantime, she indulges in her love of all things cobalt blue, dachshunds, chocolate, and of course, crafting her next historical romance.

Blue Rose Romance® LLC
collette@collettecameronbooks.com
collettecameronbooks.com

A Sensual Marriage of Convenience
Regency Historical Romance

FOR THE LOVE OF AN EARL (Wicked Earls' Club)
A Humorous Aristocrat and Wallflower
Regency Romance Adventure

HEART OF A SCOT
A Passionate Enemies to Lovers

DAUGHTERS OF DESIRE (SCANDALOUS LADIES)
A Romantic Class Difference Forced Proximity
Regency Romance with Aristocrats

A Lady's Scandalous Kiss — Book 1

No Lady for the Lord — Book 2

Love Lessons for a Lady — Book 3

His One and Only Lady — Book 4

Never a Proper Lady — Book 5

Lady Tempts a Rogue — Book 6

THE CULPEPPER MISSES
A Humorous Wallflower Family Saga
Regency Romantic Comedy

The Earl and the Spinster — Book 1

The Marquis and the Vixen — Book 2

The Lord and the Wallflower — Book 3

The Buccaneer and the Bluestocking — Book 4

The Lieutenant and the Lady — Book 5

THE HONORABLE ROGUES®
A Second Chance Redeemable Rogue
and Wallflower Regency Romance

A Kiss for a Rogue — Book 1

A Bride for a Rogue — Book 2